THE BOOK OF
BIRMINGHAM

EDITED BY KAVITA BHANOT

First published in Great Britain in 2018 by Comma Press.
commapress.co.uk

'Blind Circles' was first published in *Where Furnaces Burn* (PS Publishing, 2014).
'Exterior Paint' was first published in *Protest* (Comma Press, 2017), special thanks
to Avtar Singh Jouhl for his original consultation on this story. 'Taking
Doreen out of the Sky' was first published in *Taking Doreen out of the Sky*
(Picador, 1999). 'The Call' was first published in *The Sea in Birmingham*
(Tindal Street Fiction Group, 2013).

A CIP catalogue record of this book is available from the British Library.

ISBN: 1-910974-37-4
ISBN-13: 978-1-91097-437-7

The publisher gratefully acknowledges assistance from Arts Council England.

Supported using public funding by
**ARTS COUNCIL
ENGLAND**

Printed and bound in Great Britain by Severn, UK

Contents

Introduction

SITUATED AT THE CENTRAL crossroads of England, the city of Birmingham occupies an interesting (and not always central) position in national consciousness. It is both loved by those who know it intimately, and stereotyped or dismissed by those who don't. It has been represented in the national media under headlines like, 'White Brits set to become a minority in Birmingham,' 'Why has Birmingham become such a breeding ground for British-born terror?' and 'Is Birmingham still the gang and gun crime capital of the UK?' It has been a magnet for entirely fake news – like the infamous Birmingham Trojan Horse affair, a false story about a Birmingham-based 'Jihadist plot to take over schools' – and a symbol for the nation's fears and paranoias. Even Google gives it a bad rep: one of the first suggestions it offers when you type in 'Is Birmingham' is 'Is Birmingham safe?'

There is also of course, the perception of Birmingham as the industrial heartland of the country. The area now known as Heartlands – more familiar to non-Brummies as the haunts of the Peaky Blinders – is where the factories of the Birmingham Small Arms Company were located, which made not just small arms, but also much larger weapons, tools, parts for industrial machinery, and the cars, cycles and motorbikes that have become an ineluctable part of modern and postmodern life.

At one time connected to every other corner of the nation through a latticework of canals which facilitated the transport of raw goods in and finished goods out of the city, and across the world, Birmingham has been shaped by its industrial history

– in particular by the working-class roots of so many of its inhabitants who gave their professional lives to these industries. This working-class foundation is inseparable from the city's literature, reflected in the voices of its best-known contemporary authors: Jonathan Coe, Catherine O'Flynn, Benjamin Zephaniah, Kit de Waal, Joel Lane... to name just a few.

Meanwhile, Birmingham-based innovators, such as Matthew Boulton, James Watt and Samuel Galton, who helped power the industrial revolution, connected to the 'Midland Enlightenment', the Lunar Society and the Quakers, are all intertwined with the idea of the city, celebrated, commemorated everywhere – in plaques and statues, in the names of roads and buildings. Some of the industries they were associated with include the steam-engine, coin-minting (including for the East India Company) and gun-making.

Perhaps less well known, or less well-acknowledged, is the role that these figures played in colonialism, a role which was entangled with Birmingham's historical contribution to Britain's banking, industry, and science – not only because of the coins that were minted here, or the guns that were forged here, but also because of the workers who were later invited to fill labour shortages.

Recalling the anti-racist phrase, 'We are here, because you were there,' it is this industrial and colonial context that first brought immigrants to Birmingham; from early individual immigrants in the 18th century, to the larger waves of immigration in the 20th century: the Irish, Afro-Caribbeans (the Windrush generation whose enslaved ancestors helped build Britain), and the South Asians (Pakistani, Indian, Bangladeshi) whose homelands had been impoverished through colonial exploitation, displacement, famines and the devastation of land, trade and industries. After the Second World War, they were summoned to work in factories and foundries across Britain to help rebuild the economy.

INTRODUCTION

When they arrived in Birmingham, the new immigrants (it was the men who came first to work; later, as immigration laws started to tighten, they brought their wives and families over) were housed in pockets circling Birmingham city centre – Handsworth, Aston, Balsall Heath and Sparkbrook. They were packed in closely, enduring poor housing and living conditions, with large numbers occupying each house, often alternating both shifts in the factories and beds at home. They faced unforgiving working conditions, low pay and discrimination at every turn: this discrimination included racially biased housing policies, employment laws and trade unions, as well as colour bars in pubs, social clubs, barbers and, as Kit de Waal's story recounts, personal relationships. This is a history that later generations of writers have become increasingly interested in retracing: the experiences of first generation immigrants are the subject matter for a number of stories in this anthology; Bobby Nayyar's 'Amir Aziz' follows the set-backs and successes in the life of an eponymous entrepreneur, as recalled by an increasingly distant friend; Kit de Waal's 'Exterior Paint' recalls the racism faced by a West Indian man daring to date a white woman in 1960s Smethwick; while Sharon Duggal's 'Seep' traces the impact on an Indian teenager's life when her family opens its doors to one particular migrant factory worker.

These immigrants arrived at the tail end of industrial growth, just before British manufacturing entered its death throes. By the early 1980s many of them faced unemployment and poverty. This continues to have an impact on their communities today, along with the white working-class people who also lost their jobs when the factories and foundries started to close. Alan Beard's story 'Taking Doreen out the Sky' centres on just such a moment, joining the narrator on the day he's told his factory is to shut down.

During this period, distinct white and immigrant communities had started to form across the city. When the immigrants had first arrived, many white residents had relocated to neighbourhoods and suburbs further away from the centre. As the migrants settled, and as manufacturing jobs started to dry up, they began opening their own businesses – restaurants, shops, cinemas – changing the landscape of the areas they were living in. This settlement pattern continues to this day, with new immigrants (often from Eastern Europe) settling in the same, overcrowded inner-city locations, while many of the earlier, aspirational immigrants have since relocated outwards – to Edgbaston, Solihull, or (in the case of Amir Aziz) to Handsworth Wood.

Meanwhile, some areas of Birmingham have remained predominantly white areas; neighbourhoods that a person of colour might feel scared to enter. Here too, high rates of unemployment, poor housing, underfunding in education and healthcare, and a general lack of investment from local and national government have all combined to leave their occupants feeling abandoned. This neglect, combined with the incitement of a racist media along with the entitlement of whiteness, has meant that, in places like Kingstanding in North Birmingham, support for Brexit, the BNP, EDL, and Britain First have risen, so even the white supremacists of Joel Lane's troubling Science Fiction story 'Blind Circles' don't seem entirely fantastical. Despite being neighbourhoods that are, as Lane's racist Terry argues, difficult to live in, they are also home to communities that are genuinely tight-knit, protective and loving (of their own kind).

In the middle of this ring of complex, conflicting and often neglected neighbourhoods is the city centre: a never-ending work-in-progress, constantly in flux, endlessly undergoing 'development'. Middle to high-end cafés, bars, restaurants, shops and department stores are continually popping up across the centre, as well as around the canal developments, Brindley Place, Broad Street, the International Conference Centre (ICC) – location for this year's Conservative Party Conferences – the new train station, and Grand Central. New offices and luxury apartment blocks appear every month and, adding assertive splashes of primary colour to the city's architecture, are the distinctive, blue Bullring Shopping Centre, the equally distinctive, yellow Central Library, and the bright red Mailbox. The centre has been growing and 'developing' for years, but not without cost. As the centre has spread its reach, it has demolished more affordable housing, taking communities with it, as well as leaving many people homeless. Likewise, many iconic buildings (and the memories attached to them) have also disappeared: the old Central Library, the Pallasades and Pebble Mill. Catering primarily for the moneyed classes – including newer, wealthier immigrants – the city centre is now a space whose primary interest is facing the rest of the country, or indeed the world, like a done-up front room for guests, hoping all this expensive new furniture will finally enable Birmingham to live up to its 'second city' status.

Above the city, at junction six of the M6, there is a concrete spider web in the sky: the famous Spaghetti Junction. Meanwhile, threading through the city from below, also trickling out and away, are the canals that, designed by James Brindley, once powered Boulton's Soho Manufactory; Hockley Brook and the Tame, the local tributary of the Trent. There are patches of the canal where the homeless gather, during the day or at night, to sleep. But mostly, especially around the city centre, these canals and towpaths, lined with newly built luxury apartments, are quieter, more middle-class (largely white) places, at odds with the lively city above. For this reason, they become an apt setting for Malachi McIntosh's story 'A Game of Chess', representing his new life and a stark contrast to the figure from his past that he thinks he sees.

What strikes the outsider most of all, walking around the city centre, is how alive it feels. Locals, adapting to the never-ending 'development' and its accompanying disruption, are used to navigating its constantly changing spaces. The city derives a lot of its energy from those who have come from other parts of the world, their children and their grandchildren. (Birmingham is a youthful city, more than 40% of the population is under 25). However, although it is certainly true that this confluence of cultures, histories, and people is an important part of what makes Birmingham, the form that this takes is not the mixing and blending 'melting pot' that multiculturalism is often assumed to be. The truth is that mostly people in the centre operate as individuals, or as part of family/friendship groups consisting of those they feel a sense of belonging to; this belonging is often determined by race, religion, culture, and ethnicity. This is how people from the 'separate' pockets that surround the city centre, enter the centre. Maybe this separation (a word that I prefer to use rather than the often wielded, negative term 'segregation') is the reason people in Birmingham occupy the space so differently, and are able to express their 'difference' with confidence and creativity. It is a confidence that belies the austerity and under 'development of their neighbourhoods and the arguably bland, generic gentrification that their city centre has undergone.

The term 'segregation,' along with its accusatory counter 'integration,' has always been used to shift blame onto minority communities. The responsibility and impetus is often placed on them (Why do they segregate themselves? Why don't they integrate?) when, as the history of Birmingham shows, there was little choice regarding where immigrants were housed, where they got jobs, or where their children were schooled. Even if migrants had a choice, it is not difficult to understand why people would travel to, or want to live in, areas where there were others from their countries, towns, villages or families, areas where support could be found that government or native locals weren't able to provide – support that is evidenced in many of the stories in this collection. Nor is it difficult to understand why they might want to be close to those who understand them

– their language, culture, world view, experiences – or among those they feel a sense of belonging with. Those they don't feel insecure or inadequate beside.

It is this last point, above all, that calls into question the assumption that integration is needed or desirable. Integration, used always in reference to people of colour, is about dispersal and assimilation into a white context. Being a person of a colour in a climate of hierarchy and antagonism, can leave people powerless and isolated, taking away their confidence. Self-censorship, self-loathing, self-erasure become inevitable. I would argue that is only through separation, or a degree of it, that people can retain or recover a sense of dignity and self-respectful growth. For those who are vulnerable, it is perhaps only from a 'separated' place that creativity and resistance can flourish. Separation, a word that doesn't carry the judgement of segregation, can be a source of positivity, confidence, strength, creativity. Indeed, it is perhaps where one of the beauties of Birmingham lies.

Separate (from the city as a whole), but surrounded by those who understand them, people are able to express themselves in rich and nuanced, rooted and original ways; it is no coincidence that places like Handsworth, Smethwick, Lozells and Aston have produced such a high number of musicians and musical forms (from reggae to bhangra, gospel to soul), that have in turn reinvented the music of Jamaica or Punjab, in new contexts. Other artists – photographers, playwrights, comedians, painters – have emerged from these neighbourhoods, as well as songwriters, poets, novelists and short story writers, all producing work that roots itself profoundly to place. Some of these writers are on show here: Jendella Benson, Sharon Duggal, Bobby Nayyar, Balvinder Banga – writers who may have moved away, but were formed by, and remain inspired by the places they grew up in.

Separation enables possibilities for resistance too. Maybe this is why districts like Handsworth and Lozells have sometimes played host to uprisings (or 'riots' as the mainstream media calls them) and protest movements. Three key moments in Birmingham's resistance history offer backdrops to stories in this collection (set in 1965, 1985, and 2005), and many more featured in the stories submitted. It is perhaps because of separation that, in places like Sparkbrook and Alum Rock, after the post 9-11 wave of Islamophobia, Muslim women were able to resist collectively, while still expressing their faith, through their wearing of the hijab.

There are no hermetically sealed spaces, of course; the racism of the wider world is ever present, a constant backdrop. Racist attacks on the street, the constant surveillance of communities under anti-terror initiatives, the institutional racism (and elitism) in the police, education system, work environment and media... these have never gone away. The structures of racism abide (in Birmingham as elsewhere), disinterested, dismissive or antagonistic towards black, Muslim, working-class lives.

I'm not suggesting that these separate spaces cannot also feel suffocating and oppressive. There can be other kinds of surveillance within communities. And even these pockets are not themselves homogenous – they too divide, in response to other hierarchies, into smaller separations, on the basis of religion, race, caste, gender and sexuality. Anti-blackness, Islamophobia, casteism, classism, patriarchy – these are also all entrenched in separated communities, hence the desire to separate further, even if temporarily: separate places of worship, separate schools, separate clubs and pubs, and so forth.

All of these factors are in evidence in this anthology. Almost all the stories, set at different moments in recent history, and in different parts of the city, inhabit a contained 'separate' world – whether it is a home that welcomes South Asian immigrants who work in the foundries, or the high-rise flat of a factory worker in love with his wife, or a house party thrown by a group of Birmingham Surrealists – an informal group of artists and intellectuals who gathered here between the 1930s and 1950s. There is a sense of the wider world pressing in and how the characters might respond to it: racism in the workplace, or down the pub; the closure of a factory; the behaviour of the police. And there is also a sense of shame among those that left Birmingham behind. There are the circles within the circles, and circles that simply don't overlap. Characters view 'others' in passing from a distance: the white narrator in 'Taking Doreen out the Sky' passes by 'hoop-hatted Rastas', he looks upon turbaned men and Asian women, as incomprehensible and exotic. In Joel Lane's story 'Blind Circles', about a white supremacist gathering, this 'othering' is taken to an extreme. Occasionally, though, the circles overlap, and separate lives and worlds collide. Here the unlikely interaction that follows can be filled with fear, suspicion, even violence, but sometimes it's beautiful.

Above all, this anthology strives to give those who have grown up in Birmingham, who have lived or are living in Birmingham, the chance to represent themselves and to push back against stereotypes and derision from without. All too often the people of Birmingham have seen well-funded television crews roll into their communities looking to confirm their assumptions, looking to mock, ridicule and stereotype white working-class or Muslim communities. For example, shows such as Channel 4's 'documentary' Benefits Street, set on James Turner Street in Winston Green, or the BBC's 'sitcom' Citizen Khan set in Sparkbrook. With representations like these coming from outside, why wouldn't we want to create our own schools, our own media channels, our own temples, our own publishing houses?

One of the most significant movements in recent Birmingham literary history came from a group of Birmingham fiction writers, who shrugged off the parameters of an elitist London-centric publishing industry uninterested in their work.

The group was also a kind of separation, from the received literary culture. It was solidly rooted in context and place, in the working-class background of many of its members, and even named itself after the dead-end street on which they used to meet (at a pub): the Tindal Street Fiction Group. Four of the writers published here (including Joel Lane, who sadly passed away in 2013), and myself, were at one time, or another, members of this group, or continue to be. After two decades of running as a workshop, a publishing house emerged as a kind of offshoot, publishing, in the first instance, Alan Beard's collection of short stories *Taking Doreen from the Sky* (the title story of which appears again here). Tindal Street Press was clear and solid in its agendas, publishing stories that were firmly located in the regions, the literature that London presses ignored. Its separation from the national scene was its strength – when its uncompromising literature appeared on the national scene, it took the literary centre by surprise, winning awards and recognition. Through the many anthologies it published, it excelled in its efforts to publish short stories – giving space to and nurturing many established and newer writers, as well as offering grass-roots encouragement and support. This activity is in some ways continued through the work of Writing West Midlands – led by Jonathan Davies, who is also connected to a regional and working-class sensibility.

This anthology, bringing together both newer and more established writers, published and previously unpublished stories, reveals only a fraction of the literary excellence that has emerged, and continues to emerge, from this great, complicated city. Each story explores a particular moment and place, but these are just glimpses. No single book can ever completely capture a city's complexity. Certainly not this one's. For there are an endless number of Birminghams – circles within circles – Birminghams within Birminghams.

Kavita Bhanot
Birmingham, September 2018

Exterior Paint

Kit de Waal

THE ESTATE AGENT IS optimistic. That's what he said on the phone and now, at the front door, he offers his hand and smiles: 'Baxter. Mike Baxter. Baxter Byrne.'

Alfonse Maynard had been watching from the front room window for fifteen minutes. He saw Baxter pull up in his white car, get out and walk along Marshall Street looking up and down the road, in front gardens and back alleys, peering at the uncut hedge at number eighty-five, the shoddy porch at forty-nine and the permanent satellite dishes on every house but his own. Baxter made notes on his clipboard and tapped the side of his head with his Biro, then he rang the bell.

Alfonse leads him through the house from front to back, through the narrow hall and the two sitting rooms where no one sits, rooms that smell of air freshener, beeswax and unopened windows. In the back room at least, thyme and pepper have settled in the nap of his dralon armchair, sticky spots of coffee and rum decorate a little mahogany trolley. There's a Formica dining table and chairs for his dinner, a display cabinet for his wife, his children and grandchildren, a footstool for his bad foot, a Freeview television for the news and a black CD player for Nat King Cole.

The estate agent moves the net curtains aside to look out on the garden. 'A proper garden,' he says, 'some on the other side of the road have little more than a postage stamp. And

1

you've got a shed.' He scribbles something on his pad and taps the window frame with the tip of his pen.

'Double glazing,' he adds. 'Been here for a while have you?'

Alfonse moves aside so the estate agent can be first in the kitchen, the one Lillian had installed eight months ago, the one she used exactly five times. 'Since sixty-four,' he says. 'I used to rent it, then I bought it. My wife's idea.'

'Good, good. You'll see a handsome return on your investment then, Mr. Maynard,' says Baxter running his hand along the work surface like it's a woman's skin.

'Solid timber,' says Alfonse, knocking on the cupboard doors. 'It was my wife that wanted it. Then she died.'

Baxter doesn't turn his head, takes his time then makes his announcement in full.

'On behalf of Baxter Byrne, I would like to offer my condolences to you, Mr. Maynard. Sorry for your loss,' and Alfonse realises that for Baxter, death is a professional boon.

'You have a...' Baxter moves through the kitchen to the little toilet off the lobby. '... ah yes, downstairs cloakroom, wash hand basin, fully tiled, modern white suite.' Then back through the kitchen, noting the name of the boiler as he passes, 'Domestic hot water and central heating,' he says to himself. He motions to the staircase. 'Lead the way, Mr. Maynard.'

Alfonse shows him the little bedroom at the back with its single bed and blue eiderdown. It still has Lillian's sewing machine set up and the little vanity chair she used to scuff across the carpet to sit at it. Whatever she was sewing when the stroke knocked her backwards has been tidied away. The room is dark and lifeless and Alfonse closes the door quickly. The second bedroom lost its bed twenty years ago when Lillian declared it a dressing room. She had wardrobes built on every wall and mirrors on every door. It reminds Alfonse of a circus or somewhere you might take your child for a day out; a child that might slip your hand and run away or get lost, and the very thought of this room lately has begun to give Alfonse nightmares. So he only stands at the door and lets Baxter go in alone.

'Useful second bedroom,' he mutters, 'large double.'

The biggest bedroom overlooks the street. Why Alfonse is embarrassed to be standing in there with another man he does not know. He has tucked in the sheets and blankets as he does every morning, his shoes are out of sight, there is no dirty washing in the pink plastic laundry basket and no dirty magazines shoved under his mattress. But the room smells of man and not woman and that's enough.

'Master bedroom,' says Baxter, 'fitted wall lights, central heating radiator, telephone socket.'

Baxter measures up and is done in fifteen minutes.

'Presentation is everything, Mr. Maynard,' he says as he shakes hands again with Alfonse on the doorstep and flicks his eye towards the peeling green paint on the front door. 'Red sells.'

In his chair that evening, Alfonse cries.

The next day, the lady at B&Q helps him choose a bloody red for the front door. Lillian would have been in charge of colour but the woman that helps him is blonde like Lillian with the same good shape and easy smile.

'There you go, bab,' she says, 'September's a good month for painting. Not too cold, not too hot.'

Alfonse buys paint brushes and sandpaper and undercoat and white spirit and a new flap for the letterbox in brass with rope edging. He puts some chicken to stew in his still-new oven and reads the instructions on the tin of paint. He pours himself a little rum in an amber glass and sits back in his chair. This will be a two-day job.

The next day, Alfonse is outside early enough to watch the children go to school. All the children are brown of one shade or another, in headscarves or cornrows, and Alfonse realises that there must have been a time, just before he came from St. Kitts, when all the children on Marshall Street would have been white, when maybe there was a white man, standing at this very gate with sandpaper in his hand and his shirt sleeves rolled up, a man with a tin of green paint, watching white mothers wheel their prams round the corner to the shops. Alfonse has brought out a kitchen chair. He will work from the bottom up, first with sandpaper and then he'll paint on the undercoat.

Mr. Kang stands in his porch next door. 'You've been a stranger,' he says to Alfonse.

'Oh, I've been busy, you know. Tidying up and throwing things out. I got a valuation yesterday.'

'Good?'

'Good.'

Mr. Kang folds his arms across his chest. 'What colour?'

'Red,' says Alfonse.

'Red is for celebrations, my friend,' says Mr. Kang. 'And when you leave, it will not be a happy day.'

Alfonse nods. 'My daughter lives in Sutton Coldfield.'

Mrs. Kang and the big-eyed Kang girls cluster at his gate. They hold hands with their mother as they cross the road. Alfonse watches them go. Watches Mrs. Kang button her coat tight around the curve of her hip, into the slip of her waist and he remembers Lillian and the tip-tip of her high heels on the pavement after dark, after her shift at The Blue Gate, after everyone had gone to bed. Alfonse would be sitting at the open window with his cigarette waiting. The sound of her shoes and her voice, that's what he first loved.

Mr. Kang brings them both a cup of tea, sweet and spicy, boiled with cardamom and spice, thick with condensed milk. 'You can't have tea without biscuits, my friend,' he says and whips the lid off an enamel tin eight inches wide. Alfonse looks inside at the Jammy Dodgers, custard creams and pink iced rings. 'If they make them, we buy them,' says Mr. Kang.

Alfonse takes two chocolate bourbons. Mr. Kang takes six. He won't ask so Alfonse has to tell him.

'The man was called Baxter,' says Alfonse. 'He said to put it on for ninety-nine thousand, but I must only expect ninety-six.'

Mr. Kang whistles. 'Not bad. When did you buy it? Things must have been cheap in your time.'

Cheap. The word makes Alfonse wince. He scours at the panelled door until the scratching noise is so loud he can't hear if Mr. Kang is still talking, until he is sure that Mr. Kang has gone back inside so that when he turns around Marshall Street will be quiet again and he can remember in peace.

There are two barmaids at The Blue Gate, Lillian and Lillian's sister. They both have the same job and the same words to say to the black men that come looking for a drink after work or on Sunday afternoons when the loneliness of the long day and the pressure of four walls bears down heavy.

'Blacks round the side,' or 'Smoke Room Only.' The difference is Lillian only says it with her mouth, not with her eyes.

You only get told once, the second time you remember but this is 1965 and there are new black men every week, new reminders from the barmaids or the landlord. The first time Alfonse goes in, he opens the door to The Lounge. Everyone stops talking, stops drinking. Alfonse looks from face-to-face and sees Lillian's. She gives the slightest shake of her head and he steps backwards, outside, round the corner and in again through The Smoke Room door. She walks through the bar and is there again waiting.

'Sorry,' she whispers and then louder, 'Coloureds can only drink in The Smoke Room, sir. What'll you have?'

Alfonse takes his half a stout to the corner where the West Indians sit. They're men like himself, young in the world, young to the country and homesick. Alfonse hardly joins in the conversation, his drink is untouched. He watches Lillian pulling drinks and wiping the counter.

One of his new friends tugs on his coat sleeve. 'Listen, man, over here you don't even look, never mind touch. You want a woman, you must send for the one you leave at home. Come, man, play a hand of cards.'

Alfonse holds the Jack of diamonds and the eight of clubs. He doesn't concentrate on the game and loses nearly two shillings by the end of the night. He walks home slowly with his last cigarette, the collar high on his coat. Alfonse has only come for a few years and the truth is he's not sure if he wants his woman to come, not sure he misses her. Isn't it better that she waits in St. Kitts 'til he comes back? The last time he saw her, she shouted after him, 'Write me!' That was nine months ago. Alfonse hears the tip-tip of a woman's shoes behind him and when he turns, it's the barmaid. He waits at the corner under the lamplight and she catches up.

'You left this,' she says and holds his hat in her hand.

'Oh,' he touches his hair and then shakes his head. 'I'm not myself this evening.'

'Who are you normally then? Should I call for a policeman?' If she hadn't smiled, he would have backed away. Only last week he heard that someone, an Indian man, smacked a barmaid across the face and was being hunted by the police for assault. Alfonse wasn't there and doesn't know if it's true but isn't this how trouble starts, with the pretty face of innocence and the sound of laughter?

He puts his hand out for his hat but she perches it on her blonde beehive and laughs again. 'Does it suit me?'

'Yes,' he says. And instead of taking it off her, he taps it down at an angle so she looks like one of the girls that dance with Gene Kelly or Fred Astaire. She spins around as though she can read his mind and when she stops he reaches out to steady her.

'Whoops!' she says and grabs his arm. There is a moment then in Alfonse Maynard's life when his world tilts and he understands that something has changed.

'You better walk me home,' she says and keeps her hand on his arm directing him all the way to Marshall Street.

'But I live on this street!' he says and she winks at him.

'Yes, I know.'

She tells him she lives with her mother and her sister on the posh bit of the road that bends around the corner, number seventy-five, and that when Alfonse and his friends moved in she went to have a look. Everyone was talking about it, a house full of single men, single black men, four at least, getting up to who-knows-what. While Lillian watched the house she saw Alfonse open the front door and button his coat. And just like Alfonse's world tilted when she took his arm, Lillian told him later that her world tilted in direct proportion to the angle of his trilby as he put it on and nudged it to the side.

That night, they stop at the corner and Alfonse kisses Lillian on the cheek. They both look around in case they are seen and then Lillian kisses him back.

'We'll have to keep quiet about this and be careful,' she says, 'My Mum's a bit prejudiced.'

Alfonse agrees.

The being careful bit is harder than they expect. Sometimes, on a dark night, they twist suddenly into an entry between the terraced houses and kiss for so long that it's all Alfonse can do not to ravage Lillian there and then. He feels her slender body beneath her coat, the soft pressure of her bosom, her heart against his and he wants her like food. After six weeks, Lillian has an idea.

'You go home, Alfonse and I'll finish at The Blue Gate. I'll go to my house, pretend to go to bed and slip out when no one's looking.'

Alfonse says nothing. It was Lillian's sister that got the slap in the face from the Indian man she refused to serve. The man is still wanted by the police. There are slogans daubed on brick walls telling black people to go home. There are demonstrations by the Indian Workers' Association about the colour-bar at The Blue Gate and to top it all, Marshall Street itself is in the papers for being too full of black people. 'YOU DON'T WANT A NIGGER FOR A NEIGHBOUR' is the headline and Lillian's mother is involved somehow, part of a local crowd pushing the council for all-white streets. Alfonse knows what happens in America, black men are beaten with clubs, burned alive, hung from trees and for a lot less than sex with a white woman. This wasn't the time to let the tilt for Lillian topple him headlong into his coffin. But then again, when she kisses him, touches him and says his name….

'Alright,' he says. 'I'll wait at the window. Don't knock. I'll watch for you and come down.'

On Friday it works like a dream. On Saturday, the same. On Sunday night when Lillian finishes early, she lies down on her bed and falls asleep. Alfonse waits at the window until half past one and then oversleeps for work. On Monday night, not a day they planned to see one another, he hears shrapnel against his window just before midnight. She's grinning up at him and he takes the stairs two at a time.

'I missed you,' he says and he pulls her up the staircase.

They make love under his pink candlewick bedspread and lie in the dark with their cigarettes, her in his arms, pale and soft.

'I'm going to tell her,' says Lillian. 'We're not doing anything wrong.'

'No, no,' he says. 'Not yet.'

Christmas comes. Lillian tells him that her mother has the house full of visitors and there's not a moment Lillian can call her own. If she's not working at The Blue Gate, she's washing up and making meals. She has one cousin walking her home, another sleeping in the same bed, someone by her side day and night. Alfonse doesn't see Lillian for three whole days and he begins to wonder if she will forget about him like he has forgotten his woman in St. Kitts. He can barely recall the promises he made to her back there or the sound of her voice or whether she wore perfume. He doesn't know if she has dimples and downy hair on the back of her neck or whether the moonlight makes patterns in her eyes. Does she taste of sugar, taste of salt? Does she fit against his body like wet sand under his feet? He can't remember.

Alfonse spends Christmas Day and Boxing Day with the other boarders, sitting around their kitchen table trying to recreate the festivities of home without good rum, without fruit cake, without pepper and garlic for the small, small ham on a dry pallid bone, without stew-peas and rice and, for the first time in Alfonse's life, without the white heat of the sun.

But Lillian hasn't forgotten him. Stones scuff the window at midnight on Boxing Day and he crushes his lips on hers.

Lillian is dressing one February evening when she sits down suddenly on the bed and covers her face with her hands.

'My Mum knows,' she says.

Alfonse sits up. He doesn't reach for her or tell her not to worry. He doesn't bundle her up and kiss her face. In that moment, Alfonse thinks of himself and of the viciousness of the mother he has heard about for three long months, of her scheming with others on the street to get the blacks out and put the niggers back where they belong, on the boat home. He reads the papers each day now and listens closely to the news on the radio because everyone in the foundry, Indians,

Pakistanis, West Indians talk about how bad it is and whether it can get any worse, whether it could get like America with the Klu Klux Klan, lynchings, segregation, assassinations.

Lillian raises her head and looks at him. 'She knows, Alfonse! She's furious with me. She was screaming some terrible things.'

Alfonse lights a cigarette and lays his arm on Lillian's shoulder. 'Don't worry, Lily.'

'She said I was a slut, Alfonse. She said I was cheap.' Lillian wipes her eyes and grabs his hand.

'What shall we do?'

'We have to be more careful, that's all.'

'Careful?'

'Yes, Lily. Watch our step. I don't want no trouble.'

Lillian stands up straight. 'I see.' She pulls the belt tight on her Macintosh and feeds her slender feet into her stiletto heels. She ties her headscarf and places her handbag neatly in the crook of her arm. 'When you're ready to be a man, Alfonse Maynard, you know where to find me,' she says.

Alfonse goes to speak but the door slams so hard he's worried that it will wake the house and give the game away if there is any game left.

Alfonse sleeps not one single minute of that night. He squeezes his eyelids together and lies as still as his mourning body will allow but peace can't find him. Lily has gone. Morning comes and Alfonse doesn't move. His alarm alarms and he throws the blasted thing to the ground. Lily has left him. He smokes cigarette after cigarette until his mouth begs for water. It's Friday. Payday. Alfonse has missed his first ever day of work.

He sits up in bed and peels back the curtains. The road is quiet. He looks at the corner where he first kissed Lillian and wonders if he will ever get to kiss her again. He has to get her back.

Then Alfonse notices at the top of the road, a big group of men have gathered, some with notebooks out, some with cameras and standing in the middle of the group is a tall black man in a hat and glasses. Alfonse pushes his head out of the window as far as he can without tumbling to the ground.

'Can't be,' he whispers. 'Just can't be.'

There are two Indian men at the corner and a black woman too.

'Can't be.'

Alfonse is dressed in his trousers, shirt and socks in seventy-five seconds. He has his arms in the sleeves of his coat as he opens the front door. He stands at the gate and looks to the top of the road and the apparition.

'Can't be.'

Then suddenly the black man walks away from the crowd, just him alone. He comes down Marshall Street looking left and right at the houses, at the 'For Sale' signs in the windows and the group at the top stand and watch. Someone is filming and 'if they are filming this thing,' says Alfonse out loud, 'it's because it is true.'

The man gets closer and closer and as he walks past Alfonse, their eyes meet, black man to black man and again, Alfonse feels a shift in his world. The black man walks to the corner of the road and Alfonse has to follow.

'Malcolm X,' his heart says over and over, 'Malcolm X.'

A group of women are waiting for him at number seventy-seven. A group of white women and with them Lillian's mother. They stand in the front garden and shout, waving their arms and pointing.

'Go back home!'

'We don't want blackies here.'

'Get out of our country.'

Malcolm X doesn't turn his head, he doesn't answer, doesn't break his stride nor cower. It's as if he can't hear them, like he's thinking his own thoughts, just a man out for a stroll on a winter's afternoon. There is no jeering, no name calling. Nothing.

When Malcolm X goes back to the group at the top of the road, he faces a camera and speaks. Alfonse can't hear what he says but he knows it will be in the paper, it will be in the news, it will be all over the world that Malcolm X came to Marshall Street and walked strong with his back straight and his head high. The men slowly pack up their things, put their notebooks away and then they are all gone.

Alfonse goes back inside and straight to the kitchen. 'Malcolm X,' he says. He puts the kettle to boil and plugs in the iron. He came to England in a good suit and tie. He brings it out of the wardrobe and holds it up to the light. Yes. He cleans the nicotine from his teeth and shaves carefully, closely until his skin complains. He takes a clothes brush to his overcoat and buffs a shine on his shoes.

'Malcolm X,' he says and puts his trilby on. He nudges it down at an angle over his eye and he will never know if he really heard the next words but in his heart they are clear and true.

'Do it, Alfonse,' said Malcolm X. 'Go and do it.'

Lillian is behind the Lounge Bar at The Blue Gate. Alfonse stands in the open doorway. The talking stops. The drinking stops.

'Come, Lily!' he shouts.

Men look from him to her and back to him. Alfonse doesn't turn his head. He can't see them.

'Come!' he shouts and she darts into the back, grabs her coat and skips across the carpet.

He pulls her by the hand past Dibble Road and Topsham Road, over Holly Lane and all the way to number seventy-five. He says nothing. By the time he rings the bell, they are both panting.

'I've got a key,' Lillian whispers but before she can get it out, the door opens. Lillian's mother. She folds her arms, opens her mouth but Alfonse is quick.

'Your daughter has come for her things,' says Alfonse, calm like Malcolm X. 'Go on Lily, and then give your mother your key. You won't need it again.'

Lily slips past and the woman gasps.

'Lillian and me will be married next week,' says Alfonse. 'We would like you to come.'

Curtains move in the front windows of all the houses along Marshall Street. Women up and down the road and in the shops and in the pubs and clubs and launderettes would talk for many years about the time a black man fronted Lillian's mother and got the better of her. Alfonse would always remind people that Lillian's mother did try and speak but he held up his hand, palm to her face and said simply. 'No.'

Alfonse carried Lillian's little suitcase and a lightness in his heart that never left until Lily died.

Alfonse wipes the sanded door with white spirit. He has gone down to the wood in some places. If he was staying maybe he would strip it right back and peel off all the layers of exterior paint that have built up over the years. But he only needs to smarten it up for the sale. Presentation is everything. He will go inside now. His chicken will be stewed and ready to eat and he will pour himself a good inch of rum tonight, two good inches. Three.

He will paint the door tomorrow and afterwards he will invite Mr. Kang and his wife and the Kang girls into his home like Lily used to, when she would lay the table with all sorts of treats and sweets and sandwiches. He will buy a nice tin of biscuits from the supermarket and orange squash for the children. Alfonse will show them Lily's new kitchen and they can all sit in the front room, sit and sit until it smells of people and not furniture polish.

It's a good thing to think about the past, to think about Lily. Nine days after he walked on Marshall Street, Malcolm X is killed. Alfonse reads it in the Sunday paper and has to sit down. He tells Lily all about it, how he and Malcolm spoke heart to heart and Alfonse found the strength to stand up and be a man. Lily kisses him and says he should send a card of condolence to the widow and children. So Alfonse does. There are photographs of the funeral a few weeks later and Alfonse imagines the grief of the crying wife and wonders if she will ever recover.

Alfonse sips his white rum and knits his hands together. There is red paint under his nails. When the 'For Sale' sign goes up people will come and walk through his rooms and touch his things. They will open Lily's cupboards and look at her clothes but they will never know her and the gentle touch of her hand and the way she made him feel. 'I love you, Alfonse,' she said just before she died.

People will come and look at Lily's sewing room and the little bathroom and they will think about changing the shower curtain or replacing the roof. They will knock the two downstairs rooms into one like Mr. Kang did and they will think how much better it would be without the dralon chair and photographs of a dead woman, without the old man that lives in one room.

Alfonse holds his glass up towards heaven. 'Lily,' he says. He goes to drain his glass and then remembers and smiles. 'And Malcolm.'

Seep

Sharon Duggal

IT WAS CHACHA-JI WHO'D told Bina's father about the new boy at the factory. Her uncle said, 'He has just arrived and is not in a good home. Maybe there's room for him here?'

'Maybe,' her father said as he rolled out chapatis on top of the cold marble washstand in the kitchen.

'He seems a hard-working boy but a little arrogant perhaps, as though he shouldn't be doing factory work. It seems he's from a good family. There must be space in one of the rooms?'

Chacha-ji was right, one of the men had recently moved out and into the bedroom of an English woman in Perry Barr. No one mentioned this outright but they all knew.

Altogether there were eight rooms in the house plus two cramped kitchens, the bathroom and the outhouse. Two rooms were used as bedrooms by Bina's family: her mother, father and two babies in the room next to the front door; Bina, her sister and her younger brother in the middle room. The main kitchen was adjoined to a larger living room where the family convened and ate their meals away from the tenants. This living room contained an old-style radiogram and off-centre fireplace, above which hung a large framed print of a pale Victorian boy blowing bubbles. Often, one of the tenants would appear at the doorway of the family's living room on the pretext of some trivial matter; this was almost always when

15

the thali dishes had just been filled and hot buttered chapatis were stacked in a pile in the middle of the table. A bright sash-window overlooked a narrow side-return where hot saucepans were left to cool, and cleaning products were stored in a wooden box to save the kitchen from becoming too cluttered. Further along was the small outhouse containing a toilet and a sink; this was kept for the exclusive use of the family. The tenants shared the upstairs bathroom which had been divided by a partition wall to create a small makeshift box-like second kitchen in one half of it.

There were fourteen tenants altogether including Chacha-ji: five men slept in the large sunny first-floor bedroom overlooking the park at the front of the house and the others squeezed into four smaller bedrooms across the two upstairs floors. It was Bina's job to clean the rooms on Saturday afternoons, when the men went out to spend their scant wages in the pubs and betting shops along Soho Road. Bina liked the front bedroom best; it was the grandest in the house with a big square bay window where she could stand behind the heavy drapes and watch the English and Jamaican couples holding hands and smooching on park benches across the road. Groups of girls she vaguely recognised from her days at Sandwell Secondary could often be seen hanging around the park smoking cigarettes and, she guessed, discussing boys and what they might wear to the dance that weekend. These half-imagined, half-overheard-on-street-corner conversations perplexed Bina, alluding as they did to a world she lived amid but only ever teetered on the edge of.

Bina had once been to a club where the mystifying dances took place. It was the last term of her school days and she and her friend Krishna (the only other Indian girl in her year) told their parents they were studying together for an important exam. Instead they went to the 'Summer Special' that had been talked about at school all week. The dance was in a youth club on Soho Hill behind an insalubrious pub. It was more unexpected than Bina could have imagined. The room was low-lit and smoky and both she and her friend felt conspicuous in their long, plain shalwar kameez. They shuffled through the sweaty crowd into a dark corner to drink lemonade, watching as the girls in short skirts danced freely with boys in a way that was both shocking and fascinating at the same time. The charged atmosphere of the club with its odour of sickly-sweet deodorant and its intoxicating undulating music made the skin on Bina's arms itch and burn like nettle stings. Krishna hated the dance. She said it was grubby and obscene. She insisted they leave after less than twenty minutes. In the toilets on the way out, Bina asked one of the short-skirted dancers about the music. The girl gave her a nonchalant glance in the mirror, eyed her up and down and replenished thick lines of black kohl around both her eyes before she said, 'Don't you lot know owt? That's called Soul, it is. It's American music. All the clubs round here play it nowadays.'

Bina felt different after she'd been to the dance and for weeks she wanted to talk about it: about the American music and the way the young people danced to it, twisting and turning and swaying with their bodies pressed up close together. Krishna refused to speak about it though; she dreaded her family finding out that she'd been in a place where boys and girls danced together. The subject became a wedge between the two of them and the not-mentioning became not-speaking until eventually they just stood silently side-by-side at break-times, looking out across the concrete school yard.

The tenants in the house mostly worked long and filthy shifts in the factories and bus depots around Hockley and Handsworth. They were all men, except Najmah who lived with her quiet husband Azim in one of the two tiny attic rooms at the top of

17

the house. Najmah worked on Factory Road making school pinafores by day and, in the evenings to supplement her income, she mended the clothes of the tenants and neighbours using a Singer machine that belonged to Bina's mother, lent in return for simple sewing jobs for the family. It was no coincidence that Najmah was living in the house; she was the youngest sister of a girl called Fareeda that Bina's mother had once been friends with in their little village school near Ambala. Such connections were common in the streets around the area: people arrived unexpectedly on doorsteps at all hours with scrawled notes of addresses after arduous journeys on ships and planes. Some, like the new boy at the factory, came via buses from Liverpool or London after being tipped off about a decent family or the chance for better paid work. Najmah was a decade older than Bina and, since her arrival, Bina had noticed a softening in her mother who now had a friend she could giggle with in Punjabi like a teenager.

'Bring the boy to meet us. She's in charge,' said Bina's father, nodding towards his wife with a gentle smile. 'If she likes him we'll find a way to make room.'

Everyone knew Bina's father was a good man. He was one of the early post-colonial immigrants to arrive and settle in Birmingham in the middle of the 1950s, encouraged by his young wife to start a new life, away from the people he knew around his parents' Patiala home where they lived after their marriage. He came to England alone and sick with yearning for the wife and children he'd left behind. For almost two years he shared a dingy room in a back street of Winson Green with two other young married men. The three of them took it in turns to sleep on the only single bed, rotating from one night of relative comfort on the thin lumpy mattress to two on the unforgiving carpet-less floor, with just a blanket and newspaper to separate them from the dust and the draughts rising up through the gaps in the floorboards. Long shifts in the factory, curbed beer-drinking and a little money he received when his own father died, without warning, thousands of miles away, meant that by his fourth year in England, Bina's father had saved the money necessary to secure the house they now lived in. It took another two years for him to arrange the passage for his wife and two daughters. The three younger children were born later, in England in a stark hospital room on Dudley Road. Once the documents for the house were exchanged, Bina's father vowed that any rooms he didn't need for his own family would be reserved for eager young men like himself who had come to England on the promise of a chance, only to find that the chance was laden with desolation and deprivation. His home, he hoped, would restore something of the former dignity of the young men by offering a clean room, proper bed and the opportunity for a little human interaction in languages they didn't have to rehearse in their heads.

Chacha-ji bought the new boy to the house the following Saturday. Bina's father met them at the front door and shook the boy's hand with both his own. The boy, who was really a young man, said his name was Suresh. He was welcomed into the house like a beloved younger brother or eldest son.

'Come and meet my boss,' Bina's father said with a wink, and he ushered Suresh down the hallway and towards the living room.

Bina was shoved into the kitchen as soon as the front door closed and the men's voices began to echo down the hallway. She must remain out of sight; this was always the case when one of the male tenants came to visit, especially a new one. If the visit was unexpected and it was too late to secret away, the protocol her mother taught her was to keep her head down and her eyes averted. This was also the case for her younger sister Mala now that her hips had developed a swing like Bina's and her small breasts were unmistakable mounds beneath the loose tunics and blouses they wore.

19

Bina's mother was waiting, sat at the table with her arms folded, looking much more formidable than her tiny frame or her resolute nature warranted.

Suresh was 21 years old when he arrived in England a few weeks earlier.

'Alone?' Bina's mother asked.

'Yes, Auntie,' he replied.

Bina stood fiddling with her long plaited hair and peering into the living room to get a view of the stranger from behind a small glassed-over serving-hatch that separated the two rooms. Suresh's eyes were large and deep-set and his hair a black mop of unruly curls slicked back with some kind of oil or cream. He wasn't very tall, or very short either, and was dressed awkwardly in a stiff white shirt creased in neat lines from its packaging over which he wore a blue tweed overcoat. When Bina saw him through the little window a wave of unrelenting nausea rose up from the pit of her stomach. It was a knotted, dizzying feeling of the kind she had experienced as a young child on the long sea journey from Bombay to Liverpool almost nine years earlier. This big-eyed, neither tall nor short man on the other side of the small glass opening was the most wondrous thing she had ever seen.

'You were brave to come alone,' Bina's mother said.

'Many do,' Suresh replied,

Bina bit her bottom lip, straining to hear the conversation over the pounding in her chest.

After a few minutes she heard her mother call the young man *Putar* and Bina knew he would soon be living in the house. She let out a small squeal. Suresh looked around towards the kitchen and Bina ducked, knocking a glass to the floor in her haste.

'It's nothing,' she heard her mother say. 'Maybe wind; the back door is open.'

Bina loved Sundays. Her father always cooked on Sundays. Even before he left them behind in Patiala she remembered skipping around his ankles with her baby sister in her arms as he tried to cook over the single gas ring in the shared courtyard outside his parents' kothi door. When he left them for England, she sobbed for days until her mother scolded her: 'You are a big girl, Bina. You're almost five now and you need to help me look after your sister. You can't be doing this baby-crying all the time. Your daddy has left us to give us a better life so stop crying and play with Mala while I wash the clothes.'

In their English home she still had flashbacks to the Patiala days even though they were a lifetime away. The flashbacks were most vivid when her father cooked, humming Hindi ghazals while chopping juicy tomatoes and fierce purple onions. He pulped these into a chutney in a hefty stoneware mortar together with fresh green chilli, coriander leaves and garlic and then set it aside while he mixed up a stuffing of grated, spiced mouli to sandwich into paratha. He fried the paratha in huge dollops of butter and served the chutney on the side. When she complained that the chutney was too spicy he would respond with a chuckle.

'We are not so English to be eating the fingers of fish all the time,' he'd say.

It was in the midst of her father's loud hum and with the dense aromas of his cooking permeating the house that Suresh arrived for the second time that weekend. This time he was carrying a small brown suitcase and a cloth bag across his shoulders. Bina watched him through the thin gap in her bedroom door, transfixed by his polite smile as he greeted her mother. The nausea she had felt the day before had not completely dissipated and now resurged making her feel giddy. Her skin itched in the same way as it had done at the dance a few months earlier. That night she dreamed of Suresh, imagining the feel of his breath on her face.

Bina awoke at 6.30am just as the sky was cracking open to reveal copper streaks of dawn. She stood in silence in the twilight with the bedroom door very slightly ajar, waiting for the men to begin dashing out to work. Suresh was the last to descend.

The smell of cigarette smoke and masala chai preceded him and the glimpse she caught of him was enough to reignite a burning feeling in her stomach. For the rest of the week Bina set her alarm for an hour earlier than she would normally do for her typing class. Twice she slept through and missed him. Once she just caught the back of his blue coat disappearing out of the front door. On Friday, she woke before the alarm and smoothed her hair with a little water from the glass next to her side of the bed. She pinched her lips together in the way she had seen Najmah doing before Azim arrived home in the evenings, wrapped her maroon shawl across her body and waited. When she heard his tread on the stairs she stepped out into the hallway and then she froze, awkwardly blocking his path. They stood face-to-face for a moment before she felt her cheeks prickling with colour. She muttered a series of incoherent words, eventually shifting out of the way. He responded hurriedly in thickly accented English to what he must have interpreted as an apology.

'It's no problem,' he said and then he was gone without a backwards glance.

Bina sidled back into the bedroom with searing heat enveloping her whole body. This was the first time he had seen her face-to-face and in all her girlish excitement she hadn't even thought about how she might seem standing there in her nightclothes, clacking like a chicken.

'Bina, what are you doing? Come back to bed, it's so early,' Mala said sleepily.

Bina wished Mala was older so she could tell her the things that Suresh made her feel, but despite her developing body she knew her sister was still too young to understand. The changes this man's presence had brought to her existence were unfathomable, even to herself.

Bina waited for a sign from her mother to indicate that all the men had left the house and would not return until lunchtime, as agreed, so the rooms could be straightened. When the sign came she made her way up to the top floor where Suresh shared the second little attic room with one other man whose name she could never recall. She pressed her ear up to the door for a moment. All she could hear was the soft hum of the sewing machine across the small oblong landing. She tentatively opened the door and peered into the room as though entering it for the first time. Suresh's bed was a sturdy put-me-up on the far side of the room beneath the skylight. Bina sat on it, sweeping her hands over the blankets and flicking off minute bits of rolling tobacco from the top cover. Beside the bed was a chair which doubled up as a bedside table, over the back of which hung Suresh's blue overcoat. She stood up and opened the skylight to allow a cool spring breeze to cleanse the room of its subtle musky undertone and then she dusted and swept around the men's few belongings, careful not to disrupt any papers or their small trinkets and photographs. When the room was tidy, Bina lifted Suresh's pillow to her face, buried her nose in it and breathed in the smell of Brylcreem and tobacco. Then she put on the blue overcoat, wrapped it around her slim body and slipped her hands into the empty pockets.

It was weeks before Bina came face-to-face with Suresh again. That time had been spent orchestrating possible encounters with him that ranged from the mundane to the overblown. She would leave the house earlier than necessary to travel circuitous routes to Brooklyn Tech, staring out of windows, ready to jump off the bus in the event she might see him strolling down the busy Aldridge Road. At home, she continued to wake in time to watch him leaving for work through a gap in the bedroom door. On more than one occasion she pulled out stitches from hems or loosened darts in tunics so she could visit Najmah on the top floor in the evenings in the hope that he would see her on a visit to or from the tenants' kitchen or bathroom. Each cleaning day she repeated the routine of inhaling the smells that lingered on his pillow and trying on his overcoat, careful to replace everything exactly as she had found it. By the third week, she started putting on the overcoat as soon as she entered the room, wearing it for the duration of her time there. She imagined that some part of her would remain on the coat and that a small trace of her would seep into his dreams as he slept with the coat nearby. Bina spent hours wondering if she was filling his thoughts as much as he was filling hers; whether he too imagined them entwined at night in a dark room smooching like the brazen young couples in the park.

Then it was Bina's father's birthday. Following a family dinner with cake and candles there was to be a small get-together in the evening, to which all the tenants had been invited. There would be drinks, snacks and card games: beer and Seep to begin with and then later, when the women had retired, whisky and Blackjack. The younger children were to stay in their rooms; Mala was to look after the babies and Bina was to help fry the pakoras which would then be served by Najmah and Bina's mother. The evening was lively as expected and the men were high-spirited, aided by warm beer and the fried food. In between the early games of Seep there was back-slapping and banter and it was clear from the heightened chatter and shouts of *badaiya* that they all wished Bina's father well. Bina strained to hear distinct voices amongst the mela and when her mother left the room momentarily she asked Najmah, 'Are all the tenants here?'

'Yes, I think so. Perhaps one or two will come later. Why?'

'No reason. It's just noisy that's all,' Bina replied, trying to sound indifferent as she pushed the pakora around the karahi with a slotted spoon.

'No reason?' Najmah questioned mockingly. 'Come now, Bina, I have seen you by our attic rooms more in the last few weeks than ever before. I think you want to know if just one tenant is here, right?'

'Ssshh,' replied Bina as her mother re-entered the kitchen. Najmah giggled and Bina was simultaneously flushed with embarrassment and with relief.

'I'm going to the toilet,' she said and disappeared out the back door.

When she returned from the outhouse a few moments later the mood had changed. Her mother and Najmah stood by the glass hatch looking into the living room.

'What is it?' Bina asked.

Najmah looked at her.

'It's your tenant. He has caused a disagreement and upset your father on his special day.'

Bina's mother looked from Najmah to Bina.

'Has he said something about us?' Bina said, wishing she hadn't.

'Us? What is this *us*?' Bina's mother said sharply.

Bina felt exposed, as though her fantasies about Suresh were written across her face.

'I just meant... what has he said?'

In the living room, the alcohol-fuelled voices of the men began to pick up heat. Suresh was at the centre of the debate. He spoke clearly, his Punjabi lilt making his words melodic. At first Bina thought the ruckus was about the gambling but it transpired it was about a more serious matter.

'This Wolverhampton politician is dangerous,' Suresh was saying. 'He is causing hatred towards us on these streets. Already I've been told to carry a metal chain if I walk home after dark alone.'

'What are you talking about? You young men come to this country and make trouble just like you do at home. You've only been here five minutes and already you think you know everything,' Chacha-ji said.

'I am only repeating what I've heard at the factory,' Suresh said defensively. 'And not just from other Indians either.'

'Well this is the problem. Sometimes we just have to think about our own people and not listen to those that cause trouble. We don't need to do different things. We just have to show the English that we are not trouble-makers, that we are just here to work and make a better life.' said Chacha-ji.

'We are not their servants. We came here to rebuild their country after they tried to destroy ours. They should remember that. They should be grateful to us but instead they treat us like second-class citizens. We're only in this country because they were in ours,' Suresh replied.

'Perhaps when you have a family of your own one day you will realise that what my brother says is correct,' Bina's father said quietly.

'That is ridiculous,' Suresh replied. 'If we didn't stand up to these aggressors then our country wouldn't be independent as it is now. And in this country we still need to stand up for ourselves.'

Bina's mother tutted. 'Who does this young man think he is to speak to his elders like this? He is disrupting our household, stirring up feeling unnecessarily.' Bina and Najmah looked at each other but neither spoke. 'He won't like this talk on his birthday,' Bina's mother continued. 'It will cause bad memories. Things he left behind in India. This boy is just like he was at that age. Your chacha can see it too.'

In the living room, Azim slammed his fist on the table.

'Independent at what cost? So our communities could be torn apart and those that grew up as brothers encouraged to massacre one another?'

Najmah stared at her husband through the hatch, her eyes full of pride.

'Oh shut up with this talk. Just drink whisky and forget political matters,' chipped in one of the other tenants, slurring his words as he spoke. Other men grunted assent but the argument continued, becoming more intense.

'Maybe this boy is not a good tenant for us,' mumbled Bina's mother, glancing at Bina. 'Maybe I made a mistake. Too many things are changing since he came into our house.'

Bina looked at Najmah in alarm, silently urging her to speak up for Suresh. Najmah consented.

'He's full of the high-spirit of youth, like many his age. Azim was the same when we first married. Suresh just needs to settle into the country for longer. It's a big change for him,' she said gently and Bina was grateful.

'Maybe,' said Bina's mother over the raised voices.

The women reverted their attention to the living room via the hatch in time to see Bina's father stand up. He clinked the side of his glass with a teaspoon and the voices around him waned. Bina held her breath. When the last voice had hushed, he said, 'Suresh, that is enough now. We will have these discussions another time. You are right, there are many problems for us Indians here and at home too, but today is my birthday and I want us to forget about the streets outside and instead celebrate our household and all the people in it. Okay, my friend?'

'Yessir, of course. Apologies,' Suresh replied with what seemed to Bina to be a touching humility. In that moment he was more extraordinary to her than ever before.

'Your father is a noble man,' Bina's mother said as the women returned to their business about the kitchen. 'I pray that one day you find a man to equal him,' she added.

Najmah piled up the next batch of fresh pakora onto the empty serving plate but before she could lift it from the washstand counter, Bina whipped it up and proceeded into the living room with it held confidently in front of her.

'Bina!' her mother exclaimed but her daughter ignored

her. She placed the dish on the table in front of her father whose head was lowered as he focused on the hand of cards he had been dealt, then she turned back towards the kitchen. As she stood in the square of the doorway, she looked over her shoulder. The men were mostly distracted now: some reached for the hot crisp pakora, others shuffled cards or refilled glasses from the Party Seven beer canister on the mantelpiece. Some continued to discuss politics in hushed Punjabi and Urdu tones. Only two pairs of eyes met Bina's as she looked back: the first were her father's who glanced at her momentarily, not with the disapproval she was anticipating but with the kind of unflinching affection that always filled his face when he looked upon his children. The second set of eyes belonged to Suresh. Bina paused on the threshold with unexpected courage despite the weakness in her legs. She looked directly at Suresh hoping to see a glimmer of her own longing reflected back at her but his eyes gave nothing away. All she knew for certain was that nothing was the same anymore.

The next day, Bina rushed cleaning the rooms on the first floor so she could spend a little more time in the attic before the men returned from Soho Road. On the landing, she heard the intermittent hum of the sewing machine and the soft murmurs of Azim and Najmah escaping through their bedroom door. In Suresh's room, she put on the blue overcoat, wrapped her arms around herself in an embrace and swayed silently across the room as if the American music from the dance was playing out around her. Then she lay on Suresh's bed, put her head on his pillow and watched as clouds rapidly drifted across the skylight.

Amir Aziz

Bobby Nayyar

LATE IN AUGUST 1974, Amir Aziz broke both his ankles. The doctors said that it was a million-to-one accident; he replied that to suffer at such long odds was a blessing. He had been carrying some boxes down a metal stairwell, tripped and trapped both of his feet as he fell forward. I was there when it happened, his screams reaching out from the shop floor to the offices. The doctors had to operate; they placed metal pins in his bones. They said that it would take between four to six months for him to recover. Amir shrugged it off and tried to smile, a thin line of tears on his face. I was the only one from the factory to visit him, the others had been told to stay away while the bosses decided what to do.

Amir's wife, Fara, found it difficult to see him on a daily basis. In May of that year, she had given birth to their second daughter and was overwhelmed. She brought the two girls – Aisha and Deema – to the hospital ward, sat down and broke into tears. She didn't know how to manage the house by herself. Amir tried to make her laugh and when the tears subsided, she rapped on his chest and shrieked, 'Why can't you break your legs when you're an old man!?' Amir was twenty-four. He reached out and Fara placed Deema in his arms. He wiped a tear from his cheek and whispered a promise into the sleeping baby's ear.

Two weeks later he was discharged from the hospital. I drove him back to his house on Crockett's Road. Both of his feet were in plaster and, when he walked with crutches, they looked like they were made of concrete. Aisha was a little scared of him and hid behind her mother; he tried to laugh it off. Amir was happy to be home. His hospital stay had given him some time to think about his options: they weren't good. He had a minimal education, few friends and three mouths to feed. Manual work was his lot. He knew he would have to switch to another tack. He decided that he would become a taxi driver.

Fara laughed at him first, when he told her, then saw the steel in his eyes. She looked at his feet and Amir nodded his head. He would have to wait. The upshot of his fall was a cheque delivered by one of his bosses. The sum of money was considerable, more than enough to buy a car. Amir accepted the amount, signed some papers and waved the man goodbye, sure that he would never see him again. He tried to spend as much time as he could on his stumps, as he called them, and was soon able to do a few tasks around the house. The money had given them some breathing space and a few of his friends returned to offer a hand. When the day finally came for the casts to be removed, Amir went to the hospital alone, caught a taxi, his idea of networking. He came back home with a walking stick and a job, Fara clinging to him and laughing, said: 'You don't even know how to drive!' Amir nodded and smiled.

He was working a month later. He had bought a green Vauxhall Viva Estate and was taxiing around Handsworth and Great Barr. He worked longer hours than he had ever done at the factory, it was like the months of inactivity had given him an immense store of energy. On a cold Saturday on the cusp of spring, he came to me with two pieces of news. 'I bought a house,' he said, followed by, 'Fara is pregnant.' I congratulated him, not sure which mattered to him more. Amir was ecstatic, he couldn't keep still. We walked over to Payton Road, not far from his house to take a look at his investment. 'House' was a strong word; the place was a brick shell, gutted from the inside out, the windows missing. You could see straight into the main room and the kitchen – it was all a black charred mess. 'Are you sure about this?' I asked as he unlocked the front door. He nodded his head and gave me the grand tour. It was old and forgotten inside: two bedrooms, living room, kitchen and a bathroom, a coal cellar and an outhouse. I tried not to look worried, hoping that he planned to tear the place down and start anew.

Amir spent a few hours in the house each day, cleaning and deciding how to renovate and modernise it. Through workers at the factory he became friendly with some contractors. They did most of the building work. For a time that shell of a house, and the men who came intermittently to work on it, became a second family to Amir. I would go to his home on Crockett's Road to see him, only to greet a disappointed Fara. There were no words to be said, the look on her face was enough. She wanted my help. I made the mistake of asking my wife what I should do. Her face darkened at the thought that I was in between Fara and Amir. 'You have your own family,' she answered. I didn't talk back.

In May 1975, Fara miscarried. News spread quickly among friends and relatives, who came to the hospital to comfort her. Amir was there at first, crestfallen and silent, sat near the foot of her bed. As the number of visitors grew, he became more and more withdrawn, leaving without saying a word to his wife. Distraught that he could be so cruel, I left the hospital to look for him. I drove to the house on Payton Road. My anger subsided as I found him slumped on the floor. He told me that he had lost a son. Amir loved his daughters but never hid his desire to have a boy. In confidence, he told me that it was the measure of a man to father a son. I found it hard to sympathise. My firstborn was a boy. We sat in silence for what felt like an hour, then Amir got up and said that he was going back to the hospital.

Fara had noted her husband's absence. She returned from the hospital faded, resentful that her husband did not respond in the ways she expected. She encouraged him to continue working on the house. He accepted the encouragement on face value, feeling that if the house was a success, then all was not lost. I saw him less in the months that followed, on my wife's insistence I stopped going to the house on Crockett's Road. Towards the end of the summer, Amir called me to say that the house on Payton Road was ready.

Amir used his contacts to fill the house with Pakistani migrants, young men who weren't ready to get married, most of them recently arrived and working in warehouses and factories. He kept the rent low and fostered a good relationship with each of the men, not minding when they earned enough money and moved to better accommodation. When one left, there was usually another to take his place. A year later, he had his eye on another husk of property on Woodland Road.

It was Deema's second birthday and Amir invited a few families over for tea and cake. I took my wife, kids and a fluffy toy to their tiny house on Crockett's Road. Amir sat with me in the concrete garden and ate oranges and dates. He had never fully recovered from his accident and walked with a slight limp, his relationship with Fara had also failed to mend. They were cordial to guests but not to each other. Amir confessed that they slept in different rooms. His sad eyes betrayed the smile on his face. I placed a hand on his shoulder and looked to the low brick wall and the clothes line, our children playing unhindered all around us. Amir brightened up when we talked about the house on Woodland Road. He had bought it cheaply and was doing most of the renovation work by himself. He decided that he would rent the house to a small family. I was happy for him, glad that even though he couldn't fix his own problems, he could still think about the wellbeing of others.

A few days after a family moved into the house on

Woodland Road, Amir told me that he had bought another house, which he was planning to convert into flats. I didn't understand how he was able to keep buying properties. It was like he had secretly won the Pools. His former colleagues at work were less kind; they said he had gone into business with some money lenders, who would have no qualms about breaking his ankles again. At first I defended Amir, then I just kept silent. My wife and I kept a stable home on Station Road, but we weren't moving anywhere.

In this country where we came to live, work and die, success is a dirty word. Amir Aziz was a success and the stench of his achievements followed him around Birmingham. Some of his friends came to resent him when he moved from Crockett's Road to a bigger house in Handsworth Wood, and I admit that I found it hard to stay away from those feelings. I was the same age as him and stuck in the same job in the same factory where Amir broke his ankles. I saw him less frequently, sometimes by chance on Soho Road, other times when either of us felt that our relationship had drifted too far down the road. He called me or I called him, it didn't matter. At some point that also stopped.

By 1985, Amir owned many properties around Handsworth, all of them carefully picked and filled with warm people who worked hard for little reward. He switched his attention to the Pakistani parts of Birmingham, to Alum Rock, Sparkbrook and Moseley, and continued to buy exhausted, rundown properties. He still worked as a taxicab driver, sometimes I saw him flash down my road. He had upgraded to a red BMW 535, it was battered like his houses but moved quickly. By that time I had arthritis in my hands and knees and was working four days a week. The news I heard about Amir came from different people around Handsworth, most of it thinly veiled gossip, implying that there was something untoward about Amir's success. They would ask me why I didn't go to see him anymore. I didn't have an answer.

In 1993, I married off my eldest son. I cashed in part of my pension to afford a big wedding with a reception in the Hilton on Broad Street. I sent an invite to Amir and his family. They didn't come and although the occasion was very happy and successful, it was soured for me because of his absence. He didn't even get in touch to congratulate me. I later found out that his first daughter, Aisha, had run away from Birmingham to be with a man. My bitterness turned to guilt but I didn't try to contact him. In my time of happiness, there was little I could say to help his sadness. A few years later I heard that Amir was building some canal-side properties in the city centre. It was a big project and sure to make him a lot of money. I stopped asking about him and concentrated on my own family. I was helping my son look for a house of his own, while my wife was already asking for matches for our second son. We were still on Station Road, but we were happy enough.

The last time I saw Amir Aziz was a few years ago. I was walking with my grandson down Grove Lane. We were going to Handsworth Leisure Centre to swim. On the other side of the road I could see Amir getting out of a silver Mercedes Benz E Class, which he had parked near a pharmacy. He was wearing a navy blue suit with a white dress shirt. He had aged, much thinner than I had remembered, like he had recently been ill. He went into the shop looking hurried. I stopped in my tracks and sat my grandson on a low wall near the gates to Handsworth Park. I didn't want to continue walking and bump into him, I wanted to flee but my legs wouldn't have carried me far and I didn't want to look foolish in front of the boy. I waited by the wall and looked away from the car. When Amir drove by, I couldn't resist taking a look, I turned around to see if he would recognise me. He drove so fast, I couldn't be sure if he had seen my face. My grandson pulled at my sleeve.

'Who's that man?' he said.

'Amir Aziz,' I replied. 'He's a friend of mine.'

Taking Doreen out
of the Sky

Alan Beard

WHEN IT WAS ALL over I hung about the place to see how the next shift would take it. They mostly knew already and the Friday night clocking-on was even more subdued than usual. Me and George Brackon bandied a few words, said we'd meet at the clubhouse tomorrow. Carry on like it never happened. I watched them form groups, out of their places, some of them absently pulling on half-melted gloves. It was that quiet you could actually hear their voices.

Then I left for the bus. At the shelter I looked up at the firm's logo, the first thing to strike you about that place. Above the big glassed entrance, protruding from the wall is a model of the globe. Americas one side, Africa and Europe the other (Russia, of course, is buried in the bricks). The equator is a big steel ring with 'WE ENCOMPASS THE WORLD' printed – indented – on it. 'FALCON STEEL RINGS LTD.' is painted around this world, takes up all the earth's atmosphere. At night, as now, they spotlight the whole thing. With the blue of the sea marred by strips of red land it looks like some drunkard's bulbous eye – a bit like Brackon's.

The bus came and I went upstairs, lit a fag, and watched that world disappear. I remembered my first day there, being led by Hawkins through that swanky reception, all lights and phone-girls, to the cathedral-high factory behind. So different from the back-street hutches made of corrugated iron and breeze-block where I'd always worked, when I had a job. Here, once you'd got through the black rubber swing doors, you were confronted with a huge machine almost touching the skylight. Men in oily blue stood at various heights working it. On both sides of the aisle leading there, clumps of machinery sprouted within wire grids. Lathe arms, levers, wheels. The noise was like being attacked by an army equipped with tanks and ack-ack guns, the odd shouts and whistles seemed made of tin.

It was a chunk of paradise to me – a big firm with big wages. Falcon's had factories worldwide, steel rings being just one of many products, and they had a reputation for looking after their workers. Here, they had a canteen, they issued you with boots and overalls, they had a generous pension scheme, a complaints procedure, bonuses, and overtime available. They even had a resident doctor, for Christ's sake. I was smiling to myself as Hawkeye (as we later knew him) was telling us this at the factory entrance. Three or four years, I reckoned as we followed our new chargehand's bald patch through the towering maze, three or four years and Doreen would be opening the front door on to the street, perhaps a garden.

The bus stopped and I heard some familiar wheezing coming up the stairs. Eric's face, gone pink and pippy with cold, appeared. He made a beeline for me. He's just retired from Falcon's and wanted to know more about today's news. He asked me who the new boss thought he was.

I shook my head. 'Don' know Eric, someone out of Oxford I shouldn't wonder.'

'That's it, that's it.' Eric was excited, trembling. 'What do all these college chaps know about it when it comes down to it? I said what do they know when it comes down to it?' His old blue eyes had gone as clear as an adolescent's in that canned-tomato face. Behind his head I saw the city framed in lights – it was just dark enough to see that the Rotunda clock said 17:22.

'When I heard, it really done my fruit. What happens, I thought, what happens when they want steel rings again? What happens then?' The Fuji ad lit up green, panel after panel, disappeared into Eric's ear, went out and began again.

'Just no call for steel these days,' I said, "s all computers now.' I was tired; I didn't want to talk about it. That's why I hadn't caught the work's bus – words wouldn't reverse the closure, not now, words were no good. While Eric rambled on I glanced down at the street below, mainly boarded-up shops. Through the leafless branches of a street tree I noticed this man drag something out of a house. It turned out to be a woman, she was kicking, he pulled. Passers-by passed by.

'... the Germans, the Japs, the Asians they all patter-nise each other,' Eric was saying, 'but we don't. That's the trouble with this country; you never see a British car abroad.' His thin voice was accompanied by the sound of twigs scraping the dirt-fogged windows.

I got out in the city centre and the air was so cold it was like sucking down glass. Although not yet thirty the cold seems to hit me harder each year. The city went on regardless – busy with traffic and people and business as night came down fast above the lights – and I too wandered about, despite the cold, didn't want to go home just yet. Because of the closure I suppose, official with today's letter. Nothing new really, nothing unexpected, but all of us were up in arms to find the notice in the wage packet, sneaked in amongst the money it seemed. I thought 'Gordon' Banks, the big ginger lad who started with me, was going to hit Hawkeye, breathing that heavily he was at his chargehand. But we talked him down, out of it. It was hardly Hawkeye's fault.

Hawkeye and Banks have never hit it off, ever since that first day. Hawkeye had proudly taken us through the simple trimming operation – a machine knifed out the ragged middles of rubber seals, hot off the presses. He had brightly warned of the scalpel-sharp blade needed to produce smoothness. He had boasted of the machine's 'delicacy', and its efficiency ('1,500 a shift!'). He had explained how the seals were sent to be fitted into the steel rings. He then asked if we had any questions, rubbing his hands together as if relishing the prospect. 'Can we smoke at these poxy machines?' Banks asked, with a breath of onion you could smell above the rubber.

And a week or two later when Hawkeye was rummaging in our boxes in his quest for the perfect seal Banks said, 'Well I've learnt something boss.'

'What's that Gord?' (Hawkeye was very quick to pick up nicknames). Banks, straightening from his task and rubbing his hands in an imitation of his supervisor said very seriously, 'This: always shit on the company's time. A golden rule. Always shit on the company's time. Save it up in the mornings.'

No, Hawkeye and Banks have never been the best of mates, but violence was never a possibility until this morning.

I walked down through the arcade, polished wood, marble and posh shops (most of which were closing). I was looking for a pub but the centre's all changed since I did my pubbing in the early seventies. I followed this girl out into the dead middle of this city. Although late November, bits of drained slush in corners, she was dressed for summer and her legs flashed like skinned sticks in the forest of the muffled-up crowd. Starlings were swooping down to fill the ledges of buildings, their shrill noise stronger than the traffic. I wondered whether I'd processed as many seals as there were birds in Birmingham in my eighteen months at Falcon's (quite likely, I thought). Each seal supposedly getting us a ha'penny or so nearer the ground. I worry about Doreen cooped up with Ian inside that flat. Though she hardly complains I can see her tightening with it, it's getting to her insides, making her ill.

I got stopped on the corner of New Street by this smiling character, a Steve Davis look-alike. He gave me a leaflet which said 'Are You Upward Bound?' next to a shaky drawing of a rocket taking off. With the crowd jostling us he tried to give me the chat about God. I was having none of it. 'In a hurry,' I said, but I did glance through the leaflet as I walked off. 'PLAIN FACTS concerning your FUTURE,' it said inside. 'Either you are on a DOWNWARD course which leads to destruction or on the UPWARD path which leads to life.' I looked for the organisation – 'The Christ Mission. Coming Shortly to Your City – Malcolm Sales.' Of course, all those posters with that man's toothy face. American evangelist staring at you from buses and hoardings. Everywhere in the city. I pocketed the leaflet, figuring me and Doreen could have a giggle over it later.

I went into a phone box to ring Doreen and remembered, as I listened to our phone ring four miles away, how she broke her news to me three years ago during a hot summer. We were lying on that slope of the Lickeys that gives such a grandstand view of Birmingham. Half the city seemed to be up there in bikinis or bare chests running about or taking it easy like us. It reminded me of a painting I'd seen on a jigsaw box of Doreen's made up of brightly coloured dots of people in a park, only they wore more clothes in those days. It was so hot the air was unclear, things were shimmering. Doreen had her legs on show to brown them, her skirt hitched right up. I watched a kite soar, a tiny red slash in the sky, as she said that a baby was coming, was on its way. We lay between the blue and the green going through names. The city, far below us, seemed a strange, mysterious place in its dusty heat haze, like some technological Stonehenge.

I told Doreen I'd be home late and she said 'OK' as if it was something I do every night which it wasn't. In the background I heard the jaunty tune of the six o'clock news, and Ian's half-sentences ('Mummy wants cleaning,' I thought I heard). I waited for more and eventually she said, 'About an hour then?' I felt her – what shall I say – her pull through the wire and half regretted not going straight home. Instead I went straight into 'The Train' which I'd seen opening from the phone box.

From the outside, the pub is painted to look like a carriage. It's right in the centre and I pass it every day on my way to the real train, but this was the first time I'd been inside. It was done out like a train, the seats were the same shape and the same dirty tartan and had string racks above. I used to like trains, before I started to use them regular.

'Not exactly 'ot is it?' said the barmaid as she pulled my beer.

'Certainly isn't, 'sno joke this weather,' but I smiled anyway. She filled the pint.

'You the first-in-last-out type or just a quickie on the way home?'

'Just a quickie.'

'Thought so.'

As I took my drink and sat by the window (this too like a train's with arrows showing how far you could open before getting a draught) I thought: *Am I that easy to spot?* It's true I'm not much of a drinker now, not much of one, not like I used to be. Me and Doreen sometimes travel out to the firm's social of a Saturday (as we will tomorrow, babysitter permitting). We drink while a local pop group plays. I sit and watch the massed Falcon faces, bored or laughing, drunk or getting there, up with their partners for their Saturday night dance. Some of the women, solid arms bared in their going-out dresses, dance with fisted hands pumping as if they were kneading dough. Doreen and me sometimes have a twirl, but not if I can help it. I feel a prat: there might be someone like me watching from the Formica-top tables edging the dance area. When I'm dancing I feel I'm doing something peculiar, something insane, and the three minutes drag by... unless I'm the worse for wear and can bury myself in Doreen for an end of evening smooch. I like to get my face next to hers, taste her secrets in that flat patch of flesh behind her ear.

Usually we sit out the night with George Brackon and his wife, they're old friends of Doreen's family. Banks sometimes joins us but the Brackons don't really approve of him. I suppose I shouldn't either but we have this special link because we started on the same day. He's a clown, of the old type. He drinks and shows us his tattoos, boos the pop group, makes pyramids of half-full glasses and gets thrown out a lot. One night he dropped his trousers and set light to one of his notorious farts as a comment on Falcon's management. He puts his arm round Doreen and tells her silly jokes – 'What do you call a fast cake? Scone' – until she smiles. I wait with him for that slow grey grin of hers, it's worth waiting for, her face loses a few years and those eyes melt to chocolate.

But as I say, the Brackons don't approve, and usually we make a foursome. George sits comfortable in his Aran cardigan tucking pints into an ample belly, smelling of cigars and aftershave. He always exhales through his nose as he drinks, so that his glass is half-full of smoke. I notice these things because I get a bit bored to tell the truth, the only thing we have in common is we're both Albion fans. His wife's quiet, normally good-humoured, but sometimes she has outbursts of spleen (I think that's the right word) that tighten her face like a screw. I used to wonder if me and Doreen would end up like these two, sat in the club Saturday after Saturday. Don't get me wrong, we've had some good times there, it's just George's drink-shot, Falcon-emblem eyes that worry me. That and the belly that looks as if he's swallowed the football he's always on about. And is it possible that Doreen could end up as lemony, as tight-faced as Mrs Brackon sometimes is? Only last week I happened to mention Longdon, our shop steward, to George and she turned on me. Her glasses reflected the strip lighting behind the bar (I saw little figures move in there) as she scowled.

'Makes me think of Moscow that man does,' and she shivered in her white frilled dress.

I was shivering myself in 'The Train', there was no heating on that I could detect and the beer had cooled my insides. I drank up, waved to the barmaid, and left for the 6:45.

In the Bullring they already had Christmas music lullabying the last few commuters. I made my way through the hoop-hatted Rastas at the top of the escalator and descended smoothly downwards.

I only just made it and had to get in a non-smoker. I sat on my hands and tried not to think about it. I watched this upright bloke in a suit calculate figures in a folder balanced on his knees. Across the aisle this girl sat back, her eyes far away. That's how I like to think of Doreen. Day dreaming. When her face smoothes out, when she lets the world roll over. Like cats do on hot days. I like to watch her come out of it, slowly. At work when my body goes through its repetitive motions and the noise hums my brain to nothing, when I'm about as bored as you can get, I like to picture her like that. Sat at home, Ian fast in a nap, Dionne Warwick singing low on the player and Doreen sipping at a fag, day dreaming.

I realised I was staring at this girl, she had gone red-cheeked, so for the rest of the journey I looked out of the window. The train hurtled beneath tower blocks and the lit windows, coloured squares, looked like a game being played right across the city. We fled over dual carriageways where fleets of cars came and went, their eyes and tails alight. All those cars, somewhere buried in their engines, vitally, are a few steel rings, perhaps some that I've handled. They go into

Concorde Falcon's rings do, they go into this train I'm sitting in. But not any more, not any longer.

At the station someone had scrawled 'You Are Now Entering A Job Free Zone' which made me smile a bit.

It was trying to snow. I walked past our crumbling local ('Hot Pies' in black felt-tip), the second-hand furniture shop ('DHSS Grants Accepted' in red felt-tip) and over the bridge. The two still canals had lamplight smeared on them. I had to wait while turbanned men, sleek with black beards, loaded a van with polythened clothes from their factory, a converted cinema. Steam came out of ducts at the side. I watched a group of women in gaudy sarees clock off, pulling on anoraks and gabbling in their horse-swift language. They stood in the light spilling out of the double doors and I saw hair, lips, jewels and eyes catch that radiance. They seemed to sparkle in the damp night.

I thought Doreen might be looking down at me – perhaps bringing in washing from that oversized flowerbox which is our balcony – but I didn't check as I turned into our block.

I'd seen Peacock Towers go up when I was a kid, I haven't always lived there. (Named not after the bird but one of the councillors who commissioned them). Ever since, people have been queuing to get out. With only one kid we're a long way down the list. (Ken Saunders, who used to live above us, said that, and the tax, were the only reason he had six).

I hesitated outside our door, wheezing like Eric from the eight flights of stairs and the smell of piss. I gave one of our neighbours a smile. She went past in a fur-collared coat and old-fashioned knee-length boots, heading for the lift, muttering. I could have told her the lift was out of order but didn't, just watched her press the button and wait. I pressed our button and waited. I wanted to see Doreen open up but it was the lad from the flat below who answered. He's got these flowerpot-red eyebrows that are two arches above his glasses and I

43

noticed these first. My smile-for-Doreen left my face. All my tiredness came in a rush, I felt tipsy with it.

'Come in,' he said, 'Doreen's just putting the kid to bed.'

'Right,' I said, pushing past. I was curt to him for a bit but I knew he wouldn't get the hint. He was a young man with plans and thought everybody was interested in them.

I left him in the kitchen and went in to see Doreen and Ian. Doreen had just got him to sleep and shushed me over her shoulder. I watched her turnabout, in sweater and skirt, like a video in slow motion, finger to her lips. Her face is so familiar to me; I have watched the freckles fade and merge to give her that colour of cake, slightly under-baked. Her eyes range in colour, depending on her mood, from giraffe-blob brown to almost black. Now they moved like two pennies in their slots as they searched my face. I could tell she knew, though she said nothing.

We never kiss when we first meet, which is odd, I suppose, after four years. It's as if we have to get to know each other again each night. We stood looking down at Ian, oblivious in a fat sleep. Against the white of the pillow I noticed her zip tag stuck out of her skirt at the hip and I thought of her legs stood in the mesh of tights beneath.

'Get rid of Joe,' I hissed as we came out. That surprised her, and me.

But first we had to listen to the young man's plans again. We drank mugs of tea in the living room. The telly was on low – a documentary, there were tanks on the screen. Joe had just started as a salesman and had his future all worked out, planned like a picnic, how his wages would go up – salary he called it – his position. His thoughts worked themselves out on his cheerful face, decorated with tinted glasses and a first-growth moustache. Like everybody else he was only in Peacock Towers for a short time, he'd be out soon.

'When the commission starts rolling in. There's real money

to be made, door to door. You get the right techniques and people will buy anything. You just have to present it in the right way. The company gives you training.'

'What if people don't want the stuff?' asked Doreen.

'There's ways and means,' his lip curled as if he was winking behind those brown-tinted glasses, 'There's ways and means. I'm optimistic, I am. With the right techniques.' He liked the sound of that word and repeated it, 'techniques.'

'But isn't it wrong? I mean, pressurising some old dear out of her pension.'

Joe looked like he'd never considered this. 'I don't see it that way,' he said. He wouldn't. I thought of what Banks would say to him; he would have a go, but I couldn't be bothered. I left them to it, got up and stared at the massive gallery of windows in the block opposite. Those with curtains open showed scenes like ours – people grouped round TVs. I sometimes imagine the whole front being swung open on hinges, to reveal families in their sets of clapboard boxes, like those cages of rats you see in animal experiments on telly. I can just see some big hand coming in, picking on someone, putting them through tests.

I kept glancing back at Doreen leaning forward in her seat, listening, gently arguing her point. She was her usual self; the world could come to Doreen and she'd try and make room. I pictured her on a beach – we'd planned to go to Spain next summer – I kept thinking of that. Being there.

In a patch of silence in which you could hear the aquarium bubbling (fish are allowed pets in the Towers) Doreen nagged me with her eyes to say something. I could only think of, 'Met Ma Yates on the stairs. Now there's a character.'

'Dog rough she is,' Joe snapped in, 'nasty as a nail file.'

Doreen protested that she wasn't as bad as all that but Joe said we didn't know her like he did. 'You 'ant 'ad 'er soliciting at your door.'

At last he went and Doreen's visitor smile relaxed, small lines showed where it had been. She asked me why I was late. 'Well I gathered you hadn't won the pools when you didn't come home in a taxi.' She told me to go and eat. 'I did you burgers but they all stuck together, I couldn't get them apart.' I pictured her fingernails, which she is trying to grow, prise at the frozen meat.

I ate the warmed up dinner alone in the kitchen looking out over the clumps and cranes of the city, dotted with lights like a jumble of grounded ships. My reflection hung like a ghost over the scene.

I was thinking of Falcon's, all that space going to waste, the buildings boarded up. No more fleeing the place at 4:30, or limping back in the mornings. No more clocking-on. Falcon's would end up like the old tyre place a mile down the road, just the remains of a factory, a massive ribcage of girders dissolving in the rain.

One of Ian's pictures was sellotaped to the fridge door. Three crayoned lines – could be a waxy hand, a bush, a TV aerial. I thought that when he's older, my age, he will be in a different world and will wonder at all this fuss over steel and factory. But I try not to think of his future, don't want to burden him with other people's ambitions. My mother did that to me, pushing me through CSEs, and look where it got me. When I turned out just like dad I could almost taste her disappointment, like tealeaves on the tongue. My idea about Ian is to wait and see, but it's hard. Doreen is already picking out some vaguely professional future for him. She's been talking to my mother.

I went in, swallowing the last of the food. On telly the BBC world was busily feeding on itself. I told Doreen the factory was closing down. She said she'd read about it in the evening paper.

'What'll we do now?' she wanted to know. I shrugged,

what can you say?

'We'll get by,' is what I did say and laid my arm round her shoulders. She let it lie. She gripped my hand once, then concentrated on the film that was just starting. I did the same for a while but I was so worn out I couldn't tell you what it was about. All I remember is American accents and lots of fake blood which looked even more artificial, pulsing, because our colour balance is up the chute.

We talked a bit. I asked how Ian had been ('bombing around as usual'), if she'd been out (no – the lift was out of order). We had a bit of a barney about Joe who I put down as a money-grubber but Doreen thought I was too harsh.

'If you'd trained for something instead of drinking away your youth perhaps we wouldn't be here now,' she started and there was no answer to that. She let it drop but what she'd said seemed to hang about the room.

We both lit cigarettes, smoked together, shifted apart. We sat under our individual strings of smoke. The fish in the aquarium gawped at us.

About eleven I had a real urge for her and flicked the hair from her cheek, as if removing ash or something, getting closer to her. Her hair had the smell of apples (the new shampoo on the bath's corner, not yet stuck there by wasp-yellow drippings).

I said, 'Who's your favourite television personality?' There was an award show on and I used this to start a conversation. I wanted to get round to the question, I wanted to hear 'yes,' but I wasn't sure how.

Doreen, head down, fiddled with her wedding ring, but only managed to twist her finger (she has put on a little weight since Ian).

'Why is it closing then?' Eyes still on her hands.

'How should I know?' but I added when she looked up, 'it's this new bloke, new boss, brought in by the firm. He's streamlining.'

Doreen waited. When I didn't go on she said, 'Streamlining?' as if I'd made up the word.

'Yes you know, cutting down, the non-profit bits.' Then I said defensively, ''S not my fault.'

'But don't people still want steel rings?'

'Don't look like it. What's it say in the paper?'

'What happened then, at work?'

I sighed. 'Well there was meetings. Hawkeye took it bad' – he did, he looked like an aged and constipated Bobby Charlton – 'old "Gordon" threw a wobbly at him, near enough hit him.'

She nodded.

'A bloke from the firm came to explain the whys and the wherefores; a catalogue man, tie and everything. Very symp-a-thet-ic he was, oh yes, could see he had another job lined up.'

'What are the whys and wherefores?'

'Oh profit and that, percentages, trouble with raw materials, I couldn't follow all of it.'

'And that's it then is it? Just like that you're out of a job.' She added – 'Again.'

She didn't say 'And we're stuck here,' but that's what she meant. I said, 'Happens all the time, love. What's it say in the paper?'

'Not much.'

'Gis a look.' I was glad to turn away from those eyes, which looked both defeated and angry, going black and wet. I turned to the paper; the story was on the front page, near the bottom, under the headline '800 JOBS TO GO.'

'We got a letter,' I said and reached for my coat hanging on the arm of the sofa. The Jesus leaflet came out with the letter.

'Oh read that. 's dead funny. Malcolm Sales' lot.'

'Who?'

'You know. The evangelist, buckets of blood for sinners. On at the Villa.'

I left her reading and went to make coffee. I poked my head in to see Ian but in the gloom I could only make out the MFI chest of drawers covered in stickers. I tiptoed in and bent to kiss the dark sweat-smudged curls, a baby taste still, strange in the coloured darkness. A pure, warm taste, not wrecked yet like adults were with stuff, drink, drugs, dirt. It came to me in that room, my eyes gradually picking out toys and story-books and cartoon wallpaper, it came to me that our marriage was like that: in its infancy, not wrecked yet. Whatever might happen, it was not wrecked yet.

I listened to him sleeping until I calculated the kettle had boiled. *At least I'll see more of him,* I thought as I went back along the narrow corridor. Perhaps I'll stay with him while Doreen goes back to the supermarket, if she wants to, if they'll have her back.

I went in with the mugs to be greeted by laughter. Not Doreen's, some celebrity had cracked a joke in his acceptance speech. Doreen was reading the leaflet, the firm's letter lay on the arm and I picked it up and read it again, perhaps for the fifth time. All the time I kept glancing across at Doreen, trying to gauge her mood, but she kept her head down.

Then she asked, 'Well, are we upward or downward bound?'

'God knows,' I said and laughed for the first time today.

We drank up and went to bed. I missed Doreen's undressing; she was already in bed, sheets tight across her breasts, reading a library book when I came in from the bathroom.

We lay separately. Doreen slightly frowning at her book. The woman next door was singing, snatches of la-las, words, the song of a mother. Some nights there's screaming and fights, locked out husbands banging on doors, or loud parties, but tonight there was just the woman singing and the patter of drizzle. I felt the Falcon rhythm, 1,500 movements a day, loosen and dissolve.

Doreen turned on her side with the book. The bedclothes shifted and I saw a large area of her back, the dark hair fell at an angle across her neck and one shoulder. The other shoulder blade made a deep triangular shadow, it looked like the root of a wing. She seemed as exotic as an Asian curled next to me. I thought of holidays, of small waves being doused in the sand. Her ear was pricked, I could tell, for a move from me or perhaps Ian's bubbling cry. She put the book down, leaned to switch out the lamp.

'We will get out of here, Mark, won't we?' She said it mildly. I couldn't be sure she'd spoken. She didn't turn round.

The woman next door was still singing. In the dark Doreen's back had turned grey, it almost seemed to be transmitting like a television left on after closedown. I thought of all the days she'd lived that had brought her to this point, lying in bed beside me.

Then I stopped thinking, I slotted into her curl until I felt contact along my whole length, my arm beneath hers round the waist. She had a grassy smell of talc and babies. I had her tight and felt her warmth enter and spread in me. 'Doreen, Doreen,' I was saying before I knew it, chanting it softly like a song, 'Doreen, Doreen.'

1985

Balvinder Banga

As the shops on Lozells Road were being petrol bombed, a grandmother shuffled out of the Gurudwara on Soho Road. She was frail and stooping, still carrying Prasad when her left arm was sliced off by a black guy who mugged her for the gold bangles on her skinny wrist. Her identity was a mystery, as was that of the attacker. But we all heard from someone who knew someone who swore the story was true. You could have gone into any of the local pubs – The Grove, The Woodbine, or The Frighted Horse – and, if our lads were there, all you'd hear was talk of how they'd carve that scumbag's face and ram a gold bangle down his throat if they ever found him. They were casual words, slipped between talk of who Aston Villa were playing next and who was the fittest member of Bananarama. But still, it made you think.

I first heard the story from my cousin, Ash. He was vexed because it never made the news. 'No one cares about us, bro,' he said to me, slamming his left palm against the till at his dad's cash and carry.

Everyone was sleeping with hammers and kitchen knives, telling their mothers and sisters, 'Best to stay in until it cools down a bit.' Sarwaran Uncle, Ash's dad, had gone into his loft and got down a three-foot sword he had bought in Amritsar eight years ago. He polished the blade with emery cloth and hung it in his living room.

At our house, I put a Stanley knife under my bed and placed a homemade nunchaku with a rusty chisel on the front room settee. If anyone had looked through the net curtain they would have known I was ready to spill blood for my family.

My mum had glared at me, saying, 'It looks as if criminals live here. Move the picture of Guru Gobind Singh to face the front door. The Guru is the best protection.'

'OK,' I said while she started putting on her chunni and brown coat, as if everything was fine now that the picture was being moved. 'You are doing that to annoy me,' I said. 'The Guru can't protect you if you walk alone to the Gurudwara every day. Haven't you heard about the woman who got her arm chopped off?'

My blood was pumping at her craziness. 'Dad, come quickly,' I called into the next room. My father dragged himself away from watching the news on our old, busted television with a metal hanger sticking out the back. He was addicted to it now the riots had started. 'You tell Mum. She won't listen to me,' I said.

Dad sighed. '*Jagiro*, listen to him. It's the only sense he's ever spoken.' She stared at my dad and me, and then stepped back from the front door, taking off her coat.

'You talk like a man now,' she said and walked into the kitchen with her head down as if I had slapped her. The next day, my mum told me that I sounded like my granddad when he told her stories about India's partition. She had been a scared little girl who hadn't made her first roti. 'He also wanted to protect his mother when men with knives came looking,' she whispered. 'Your voice is just like his.'

'It's different now,' I said, my blood pumping at my own craziness. I would have chiselled someone if they ever tried to hurt her.

A few days later, Ash came to our house to vent. The veins on his neck were bulging. Sitting on our settee, he kept saying: 'Someone needs to pay,' and talking about how Guru Gobind Singh was a warrior, how he was a Sikh, how we were all family. On and on he went until I had to tell him to chill out. 'You are going crazy spouting this stuff all the time.'

'I'm crazy? You're the one that's acting like this is normal. Do you think Thatcher would let Sutton Coldfield or Edgbaston burn up? Only in Handsworth,' he said shaking his head.

After that visit, Ash started to wear Karas on his wrists. They were as thick as bicycle chains with grooves cut into them in case they needed to double up as knuckle dusters. Our cousin, Parmar, who was down from Southall for a football tournament, had brought nineteen of them. 'Give them out at the cash and carry to our lads,' he'd said. Ash had nodded and stored a bunch under the counter, dishing them out with his dad's blessing. That's how I got one.

The Karas were some serious pieces of Sheffield steel on our Sikh wrists, letting everyone know not to mess with us. Ash and I were walking a bit taller while some of the lads from our Desi five-a-side football club were shrinking. They would say, 'Let's go drinking on Corporation Street. The pubs in Handsworth are battered.' Who were they kidding? They were just a bunch of scared pussies, worried in case something kicked off.

'You do what you want,' Ash would say to them. 'I'm stopping on Soho Road.'

I would nod. 'Me too. I better look after him. You know what a lightweight he is.' Everyone laughed because Ash was nearly a year older and a foot wider than me. And he could drink a gallon more than just about anyone.

I would have followed Ash anywhere. Even down Soho Road where everyone was walking about with flick knives in their back pockets and wanted you to know it. Every rude-boy hanging outside a pub had a look telling you: 'Don't mess with me or I will stab you.' They stood against walls on Grove Lane and Rookery Road, bottles of Becks in their hands and roll-ups jammed between their lips, laughing as you walked past, daring you to turn around or slow down. I would have wrestled my mum to the ground before letting her walk past them to the Gurudwara by herself. I was on edge, thinking that something bad could happen at any second. Maybe I should have spent the £20 on the butterfly knife I had been offered at New Street Station by some guy who had clearly researched his target market.

Five days after I was offered that blade, the BBC got bored of flying bricks and got a bunch of ethnic Handsworth 'experts' talking about 'making a new start for the community' as if they had ever been on Soho Road. By then, the shutters on the Lloyds Chemist on Grove Lane had been replaced so girls couldn't help themselves to hairspray or boys to the Hai Karate aftershave that we all wore until we could afford trips to Rackhams.

Ash and I had been wearing our new Karas for at least a week by then and Sarwaran Uncle had eased back into giving everyone his views on the cricket. He'd chucked his plastic Casio watch back in the storeroom and started wearing his Rolex again, the one Ash had got for him from the rag market for £100. 'If someone's going to take it, then Ash can do double shifts to get me a new one,' he said, smiling at me.

His cash and carry was still closing early at four o'clock every day – as it had been ever since the first BBC report of shops getting smashed in Lozells. That was only two weeks ago. It felt like we had been under siege for a year.

There were still a couple of baseball bats under the checkout, one for Sarwaran Uncle and one for Ash, but all the Karas had been given out days ago. Ash's talk of getting a shooter had dried up. I had said to his dad, 'Uncle, say the word. I can drive to Southall and get something small to hide under the till. I know Ash has to stay at the cash and carry, but I'm at college. My teachers at Matthew Boulton wouldn't know if I took a day off.'

Ash was all for the idea. He kept saying to his dad and me: 'If all this rioting is political stuff about some black guy getting arrested then why are they coming down Soho Road smashing our windows? You don't see them targeting the Jamaica Food Hall. We need to protect ourselves.'

Sawaran Uncle talked over him, acting like only I was standing next to him. He grabbed me by the neck and pulled me towards him. 'Son, the only thing I want you to get from Southall is a wife for this one,' he said and then slapped Ash on the back. It was an old joke, but I laughed harder than ever.

'Hear that. Your dad knows you need *me* to find you a woman.' We both looked at each other trying to get a hint of what the other was thinking. Had Ash calmed down or not? I didn't know. He was smiling but refusing to look me or his dad in the eyes.

By the time the cash and carry had been locked up, it was nearly five. Ash said he wanted to go for a drink. 'I'm with you,' I said, as always.

Sarwaran Uncle walked over to us and said, 'Why don't you two come home instead? I'd rather you had a drink with me, so I know you are safe. And you can have some roti.'

I told him that I would eat roti at his house some other time. He eventually relented and passed a tenner to Ash: 'Get something at the KFC for him. I can't have my son going hungry. And you calm down,' he said, cupping Ash's chin in his hands before driving off in his Ford Transit.

Ash and I stood on Soho Road and waved goodbye to him. I was shivering in my Ralph Lauren shirt. My sleeves were rolled up and I wore my fat Kara on my wrist for the whole of Handsworth to see. They had to know who I was. I was Sikh. Sikhs weren't going anywhere and Guru Gobind Singh was a warrior. Udham Singh was a martyr. It was different now. We didn't need to hide like my mum had when she was a kid during partition. Soho Road was ours.

Even before that evening, for several days, these thoughts had been punching my brain until I started stealing shots of my dad's Bacardi before bed, too punch drunk to think of buying a bottle of Johnnie Walker and hiding it in my room. The idea of being a Sikh ready to stand his ground, to honour his past, had become an obsession. I knew Ash felt the same way as he stood next to me on Soho Road in a t-shirt and jeans with an orange handkerchief hanging out of his back pocket. He looked fierce, rolling his neck and shoulders as if he was limbering up for a sparring session. 'Quit the Marvin Hagler routine,' I said, hoping he was just sore from working the dumbbells.

'Well,' said Ash. 'Where to?'

It was a dumb question. There was only one place on Soho Road playing music worth listening to. 'Let's go to The Frighted Horse,' I said.

As we walked in, Sonia, the barmaid, placed a couple of cans of Kestrel on the counter and smiled. I paid her and she brought them over to where we were sitting.

'We don't need glasses,' I said. It looked fierce to have the cans on the table, so everyone could see we were drinking proper stuff, not your 4% alcohol rubbish. Three hours later, we were still there. The pub was buzzing. Everyone was watching the growing pile of Kestrel cans we were heaping around us. It was craziness. There must have been ten of them on the table. Sonia had left them there for all the other punters to see. They looked good, but I was too drunk to care by then. I could hardly hear anything. 'Come again, bro,' I kept saying. Ash was getting louder, but it was as if he was miming out of sync to the sound of Gregory Isaacs being pumped through the jukebox. The beer in people's glasses was shaking with the reverberation of the base. My bro was teary, slamming his left palm on the table, saying: 'We shouldn't forget we are warriors. She was coming from a Gurudwara.' It had barely turned eight o'clock.

People started looking at us, not at the empty cans of Kestrel. Maybe they always were, waiting to piss themselves laughing if we got too drunk and threw up on the table.

'Donny from the bakery says the man had a machete,' Ash said. 'The bastard!'

He carried on talking while I felt the room go cold for a second. Sonia walked over and said: 'That's your last one, boys.' She went back behind the bar and talked to one of the regulars, a black guy who looked ripped even through his Aston Villa sweatshirt.

'OK, Hector. Keep safe,' she said.

Hector nodded to her and placed his empty glass on the bar. He then turned towards Ash and leaned in: 'You keep mouthing that shit and you'll be the one getting busted open.' He said it loud enough for everyone to hear. Sonia spun around, turning her back to us. Hector then walked out the door before I could explain to Ash what he had said. He was still busy telling me what other news Donny had to offer.

'What!' he said, when I finally got him to shut up.

'Hector knows people,' I said. 'You know he got Avtar sliced. Our boy got seven stitches to his forehead because he slapped up one of Hector's mates who tried to mug him.'

'Bullshit. Avtar told me himself he got those stitches from fighting outside The Dome. The man can't handle his drink when he goes clubbing.'

'Whatever. And anyway, Sonia said we should drink up and get lost.'

'Cheeky cow,' he muttered, slowly sipping his Kestrel for another ten minutes. I knew he wouldn't risk getting barred by telling Sonia what he thought of her. He had learnt that lesson the hard way last year. I was hoping he was too drunk to remember that Hector had threatened him because if he did, it was never going to end with a few slaps, like when we were kids scrapping in Handsworth Park. I watched him drain the last dregs from his can and then said, 'Come on, bro. We need some KFC to soak up the booze.'

'Give me a minute,' he said before getting up and walking over to some guy by the jukebox who was minding his own business with a pint of Carling. The two of them left the room together and returned a few moments later.

'Just a bit of business,' said Ash. I was too drunk to ask what business he had to do. I assumed he was buying a spliff for later. I got up and followed Ash into the fresh air, sucking it in to sober up a little.

We got a family bucket of chicken, two one-litre bottles of coke and sat in his Ford Escort, filling it with the stink of fried chicken and Pepsi belching out. Ash downed three-quarters of his bottle in one go and then switched on the ignition to heat the car up.

'Give me the rubbish,' I said and got out to walk the three feet to the bin outside S&D Supermarket. Its shutters had new graffiti on them. There was a dent in the steel that could have taken my whole fist. I looked at Ash and said: 'Jeez, you can see the brick that struck it,' expecting to hear some more talk about how one day, if things didn't change, there was going to be a war in Handsworth, and not just scuffles with a few bricks and petrol bombs, a real war with blacks and Indians shooting each other up.

'Wait and see,' Ash would usually say. 'They will bring their boys from wherever. We'll bring ours from Southall. When one of them falls the BBC will talk about peace and love, and community relations. When one of us goes down it won't even make it to radio, let alone the TV. They don't care about us, bro.'

Ever since the riots kicked off he'd been saying this stuff all the time. All that talk of war, it was like the bullshit one-liners Tony Montana off *Scarface* spouted. But Ash didn't say anything, not that time. He just sat there, not really blinking, staring out of the windscreen.

I got back in the car. 'I'm ready for bed,' I said and waited for him to rip into me because I couldn't hold my drink. Ash wasn't in the mood for joking though. All he said was: 'Who did he say would get busted up?'

'You're thinking about that fool? Forget Hector. He knows shit,' I said, shaking my head. Ash reversed gently out of the parking space.

'Ready? 'he said, and then floored the gas pedal, scraping the kerb as he bombed out of the car park on the Nineveh Road exit.

'Why are you heading towards Winson Green? Slow down, bro.'

Ash was driving like a bandar, a monkey. 'Chasing the dumb shit isn't worth it,' I said, smacking the glove compartment. 'We're in a Ford Escort. It's not KITT. Screwing a spoiler on the back doesn't make you Knight Rider.' For a second he looked at me and laughed, his right fist crushing the orange cloth he had wrapped on the steering wheel to soup it up a bit. I was scared of him, but said it anyway.

'Look at the road!' I shouted, and he laughed again.

'When have I ever let anything happen to you?' he said. He was right as well. Ever since we were kids he'd been eyeballing anyone who looked at me funny. But that didn't change the fact that I could smell the hot tyres scraping a kerb.

'Can't you smell it? You're mashing your tyres up,' I said, thinking I was about to chuck up a bucket of KFC as he rammed them up the pavement for the sake of some black guy who I knew he could spark out *whenever* he wanted to. 'Quit the Tony Montana bullshit. You're not in *Scarface* bro. It's Nineveh Road. Slow down.'

'You're my brethren,' he said, his eyes glazing over.

'Wake the fuck up!' I said and sucked my lips, seeing then that he wasn't blinking. 'That isn't spliff. What is it?'

I knew he had taken something. When he did stuff like this he would say it was to 'flick the switch' because things were a bit heavy. I knew that was rubbish he spouted because he wanted to sound like a gangster. He used Al Pachino one-liners all the time. He even wore a white suit for a few days – until one of the aunties pulling a shopping trolley at Badials laughed at him. 'Son,' she had said, 'my husband had a suit like that when he came to Birmingham in the 1960s.' I had slapped his back and started laughing as I paid for the 25-kilo sack of Chapatti flour we had gone to get. That seemed a long time ago now.

★

Whenever Ash used to talk of 'flicking the switch' he would scare me. Whenever he got that zombie stare in his eyes he would scare me. Whenever he did something stupid, which was all the damn time, he would scare me. I spent half my time with him worried in case he killed someone or got himself killed. I loved him. He was my brethren. He *is* my brethren, but the man was insane. Whenever the screws flew out of his brain, it was me that had to fix them back in. I would call him a stupid bandar, make him drink water and try to snap him out of it. What else could I do? My heart still smashes against my ribs thinking about the time at The Frighted Horse when his eyes had swivelled into his head and he'd started shaking. That was nearly six months before the riots started. I'd had to pull him, moaning and retching, into the back of his car and drive him to Dudley Road hospital. The doctors had to pump his stomach because he was stupid enough to down a Bacardi shot with something that was meant to be a vitamin pill for a horse.

I remember Ash had been chatting to some random guy who kept calling himself his brother. 'Don't you know our dads go to the same Gurudwara? They came from the same village, bro,' the man had said while laughing at Ash.

It had been near closing time and Ash was slurring his words and dabbing his eyes with a tissue from his pocket. All Sikhs were family then, and if someone called you bhaiji, brother, a few times, you would empty your pockets for him. That's what this scum, Pritu, did. Bhaiji this. Bhaiji that. Yeah, same again is fine, bhaiji. Don't bother with crisps, bhaiji. And then Pritu gave him the horse pill, as if anyone in Handsworth had ever been anywhere near a horse.

Pritu's eyes didn't waver, staying on Ash as he told him: 'It's better than a protein shake if you're bulking up. How much power must it have to get a stallion to do a grand national? Think about it.'

'A tenner for two of them,' Ash had said before shaking Pritu's hand. It was the sort of crazy thing Tony Montana would have done.

Ash spent three days in the hospital waiting for the all clear, for the horse pill crap, or whatever it was, to leave his system. In all that time, his eyes were glazed, popping out like marbles, while his mother was holding my hand, telling me: 'You saved him. You are my own flesh as much as he is. My son.'

'He's my brother,' I mumbled, staring at my Adidas Sambas and cursing myself for not slapping Pritu when I had the chance.

On Ash's second night in hospital, I walked into The Frighted Horse and shouted: 'Where is the bastard, Pritu?' I'd already seen him at the bar but wanted everyone to know I was settling family business. What kind of man would I have been if I had let scum like Pritu put my brethren in hospital without a consequence? Sonia had already turned to face the dart board as I dragged Pritu by his oily hair out of the side entrance of The Frighted Horse. I dumped him on Stafford Road with a broken nose and a couple of gashes in his forehead from my sovereign ring, the one with *Ik Onkar* written on it. He was still saying 'bhaiji' as he knelt on the pavement with me punching him, trying to avoid his blood on my Tommy Hilfiger t-shirt: 'Sorry, bhaiji. Hector gave them to me. Forgive me, please.'

I stopped punching him for a second, breathing heavily. If he had named anyone else I would have hunted them down with a baseball bat, but Hector was untouchable within a five-mile radius of Soho Road. Pritu must have thought Hector's name would act as a gum shield. 'Bhaiji, please,' he mumbled with blood seeping out through his mouth.

'I'm not your fuckin' bhaiji,' I said and booted him so hard on his left hip that I could feel pain shooting through my right ankle. I thought I'd cracked it until I walked off the limp on my way home.

No one, including the cops that drove by like they were kerb-crawlers, saw anything unusual. Cops did nothing when one of our old girls had an arm chopped off. They were hardly going to stop because some oily scum like Pritu got a few slaps. The closer you are to Soho Road the worse your eye-sight gets.

*

Dudley Road hospital, horse pills and scumbags that sold them: I had hoped that was all in the past. But there I was, sitting next to Ash in his car, my hands sweating as they gripped my thighs. It was too much for me.

'Come on, bro. Let's go home. We're done here,' I said,

wanting to throw up, if only to clear the space in my throat to scream. I kept staring at his face, wishing I hadn't gone out that evening. No. That's not true. I deserve a slap for saying it, but I wished that I hadn't gone out with Ash that evening. I should have settled for going drinking with the lads from the five-a-side team, even with all their bullshit talk of drinking in the city centre.

We were near the prison before Ash turned the car around and floored the gas pedal again. He was doing 50mph over the speed bumps. 'You think you are going to find him now? Let's go home, bro. We're both drunk.' I was convinced he wouldn't find Hector, that we would go home, wake up with our heads thumping. Then tomorrow, I would start the job of cooling him down before he exploded. I was saying whatever came into my head. Before I knew it, we were back on Soho Road in fifth gear, heading towards the Hockley Flyover. For a second I thought he was going home and breathed out, but then I understood what was happening.

'It's craziness! Don't go down Lozells Road,' I said. As it was, he didn't need to because there was Hector, walking slowly past the bookies with cigarette smoke rising above his afro like a halo. 'What are you going to do? Drive back,' I said as the car skidded to a halt and Ash jumped out. He sprinted the twenty metres towards Hector with a steering wheel lock in his right hand. I must have been too drunk to have noticed him pick it up. I started praying, frozen in my seat, watching as Ash got within a metre of Hector.

'Don't let him do it,' I said in my head as Ash steamed forward. 'I'm busting you open,' he shouted. Hector's head was turning towards Ash just as the steel lock smashed in the middle of his shoulder blades. I heard the crunch from the car. Hector fell forward. I thought he was sparked out and ready for his coffin. He didn't move. But then he grunted as if he was going to throw up. He spat a cigarette from his split lips and all I could think of was how strange it was that he had kept it in his mouth for so long.

Ash ran straight back to the car, his eyes looking as if they were about to jump from his head. I had sobered up by then and got into the driver's seat. 'Get in,' I screamed as Ash threw the steering wheel lock on the back seat and started to close the door. I had already taken off. I headed towards Hockley before turning the car around and driving through some rough looking side streets back to Winston Green. I screeched to a halt next to a patch of razed grass near the canal and told Ash to get rid of the lock.

'Where?' he said.

'Come on, bro. In the water. Let it sink in there.'

'You know I love you, bro?' he said and ran to the canal with me sweating because some kids were smoking by a wall nearby. I told myself they were glue sniffers on smack, about to keel over from cheap vodka, anything to make myself believe they couldn't see us. It was all bullshit. They were just kids having a smoke, watching the world go by, watching us.

I took Ash back to my house. We were both shaking, wondering if the cops would come for us. Maybe the worry of waiting for them was worse than if they had grabbed us and taken us to Thornhill Road Station. Ash and I just sat in my room telling each other: 'We should get some sleep.' We drank glass after glass of water, thinking that we needed to sober up in case someone knocked on the door for us, to take us for an interview in a cell. I looked at Ash and thought, *You idiot. What have you done?* It wasn't even ten o'clock.

For the next two weeks we dodged the pubs on Soho Road, choosing to hide behind his front door or mine, telling ourselves, 'The lads are right to drink in the city centre. Handsworth pubs are all battered.' I bought the *Evening Mail* every day thinking that they would mention Hector, looking for news of the Villa when I saw they had not. The stress was killing me. When I had to go to college, or the Gurudwara to get my mum, I walked with my hands in my pockets, wrapping spare Karas around my fists, worrying that someone would slice me at any second.

In the evenings I was smoking spliff while Ash drank Johnnie Walker that he would smuggle into my room in his Slazenger gym bag. He didn't even look as if he was enjoying it. Half the time he'd just be staring at his glass until I tapped his arm to point out what was happening in *Ghostbusters* or whatever other crap video we were watching. 'See that,' I would say every two minutes, not wanting it to go quiet in case he started talking about all I ever thought about now: what happened to Hector and when was he coming to find us? I had been dreaming of Hector smashing a crow bar in Ash's head, calling for me in college, dragging me from a full classroom. What would he do to me then? I'd wake up before I found out. That was the worst bit.

One evening, Ash suggested we go to Gurudwara on Sunday, if only to show we weren't in hiding. He'd been going on about it for three or four days. 'You've never been before unless there's a wedding there,' I said but he kept mentioning it.

'Chill out, bro. Sure, I'll come if you think it will help,' I replied, unable to read his face, not knowing if he was cracking up like I was. I needed him to be the cousin that pumped 30-kilo dumbbells and spoke about Guru Gobind Singh being a warrior because that was just like saying *he* was a warrior and that he would look out for me like he always had.

My mum loved the idea of going to the Gurudwara. 'You have to come to make sure he doesn't run into the road,' Ash said to her, pointing at me.

'You mustn't joke about him being a child. He has a tantrum when you do that,' my mum said, and laughed with

Ash. 'Such a good boy' she added, her look asking me: *Do you think my wonderful nephew ever argues with his mother and would ever allow a chisel on his front room settee?* I rolled my eyes, glad to hear laughter in the house again – even if it was at my expense.

The Gurudwara was packed. Kids were running around, laughing and playing conkers outside like I used to do. My mum got out of the car and dashed inside the building after telling me: 'Now I can breathe. The air is so pure here.'

'We'll be in in a minute,' I said, spotting someone I knew in the crowd gathered in the car park.

Standing with a wedding party in a shiny blue suit was Pritu. He saw me, stopped talking to the man next to him and turned away, marching towards Soho Road. I ran up to him before he used the kerb as starting blocks and put my hands on his shoulders, digging my fingers into his collarbones.

'Chill out, bhaiji. You know we are all brothers here,' I said. 'Tell me some other time why your nose looks bent.' Ash came up behind us and started rolling his Karas down off his wrists. 'I want to know if you've been to The Frighted Horse recently,' I said.

'I don't go out much' said Pritu, looking at Ash and trying to step back into the speeding cars with my hands still gripping his shoulders.

'There's traffic there, *bhaiji*. You still pimping Hector's horse vitamins?' I asked.

'I haven't seen him for weeks.'

'It isn't me that's going to break your skinny neck unless you do better than that.'

Pritu looked at the Karas in Ash's hands and then spurted out: 'His brother says he's moved to London.'

'London. Did you hear that, bro?'

I took the words in for a second and then let go of Pritu's shoulders, pushing him away. 'Disappear,' I said and Pritu stumbled away, vanishing into the wedding party from which he had come.

Ash put his Karas back on his wrists. We looked at each other, understanding that Hector had survived. He had chosen to walk away from the second round with Ash that *had* to have happened if he had stayed in Handsworth. One of them would have been killed. I knew it in my gut and no amount of spliff or Bacardi had let me sleep because of it. Hector had got lucky. So had Ash, and he knew it. I could tell from the way he was taking deep breaths and shaking his head from side to side.

'You OK?' I said, holding the back of his neck in my palms, feeling like his dad. 'It's over. Hector's gone. You hear me? It's over.'

'I need to sit down,' Ash mumbled, turning his face from me and walking into the Gurudwara.

'I'll see you in there,' I said, letting him go, wanting him to go. I needed to remember what it was like before we synchronised our bravado, with all its feigned indifference to whether Hector should ever step out from his Datsun Cherry and seek his revenge. For a moment I felt as if some force had pulled me from a prison cell. I looked at the open doorway, placing my palms on my chest, feeling the sweat on it cool and dampen my shirt. My eyes were wet too by then. I rolled down my sleeves to wipe them before going into the warmth, not caring to roll them up again.

Ash was in the back of the Gurudwara's main hall, sitting cross-legged on the floor. His wrists were limp on his knees, as if they were too weak to carry the weight of the fat Karas on them. He looked like a boy, shrunken by the past weeks. I hesitated before walking towards him and then sitting by his side, in silence. I had nothing to say to him.

Kindling

Jendella Benson

THE STREETS WERE EMPTY now that the riot had come and gone. But to Lauren it still felt like the city was burning. The only sound she could hear was the soft beat of her bag against the back of her left thigh, punctuating each step. She adjusted the strap slung across her shoulders, changing the bag's position and silencing its rhythm. As she walked down her road, she imagined the gangs of volatile young men at home dressing their bruised knuckles, getting ready to return to school and work the next day.

Rumours about the Sikh taxi driver burned alive in his minicab had sent warnings ricocheting around the community. Mobs were said to be out on the streets seeking retribution by dragging unsuspecting black motorists from their cars at traffic lights. No one seemed to know for definite if either story were true – like how no one knew for definite if the incident that triggered the unrest had actually happened – but either way, the stories had been the fuel that caused the streets to blaze.

The shrill tone of Lauren's mobile phone sliced through the quiet.

'Lauren, where are you?' It was her mother. 'I called the house phone twice and you didn't pick up!'

'Oh, yeah... I just had to quickly go Melissa's 'cause, erm, she has a textbook I need for an assignment that's due tomorrow.' She was getting better at lying.

'You can't go to Melissa's, it's not safe. Wait until we get back and we'll give you a lift.'

'I've already left, Mum, and it's only round the corner anyways.'

Her mother paused.

'You said you weren't well enough to come to church with us, but you somehow found the energy to go see your friend?'

'I'm feeling better now, ennit?' Lauren's ears burned. Her mother sighed.

'Call me when you get there so I know you're safe. We'll pick you up on the way back.'

'OK. Bye, Mum.'

Her first hurdle cleared, Lauren found the last message she'd received from Zee and tapped out a reply:

On ma way xox

A few seconds later her phone chimed with his response.

Orite. Inabit.

She didn't like the way he typed 'orite', instead of 'alright' or even 'alrite'. 'Orite' sounded like 'oh, right', which felt to her like a sigh of resignation rather than genuine enthusiasm. She also didn't like the fact that he never signed his texts with an 'x', but still, there was so much else to like about Zee. First of all, he was quite tall. Lauren didn't know if she had a 'type' yet, but if she did – or if she was developing one – tall would definitely feature on that checklist. She remembered the way he had sauntered onto the top deck of the No. 11 bus the first time she had seen him. He walked erect, chest out, shoulders stiff, the waxed peaks of his hair almost brushing the ceiling of the bus. He sat across the aisle from her, one row back, and every now and again she was sure she could feel the heat of his gaze rest on her briefly. As the upper deck emptied out she heard him clear his throat.

'Excuse me?'

She turned to look at him in anticipation.

'You're really pretty, y'know,' he began casually, the absent-minded tapping of his lighter against the seat in front of him the only thing betraying his nerves.

She smiled and said, 'Thank you', not sure how to prolong the conversation.

'Can I ask you your name?'

'It's Lauren.'

'Nice to meet you, Lauren,' he tilted his head. 'I'm Zee, ennit.'

'Nice to meet you, too.'

The conversation ambled along self-consciously. They exchanged superficial details: the colleges they were at, what subjects they studied, and where they lived. He teased and flirted, easing into a confident swagger that made her skin tingle.

'This is me,' Zee said as the double decker approached the green bus stand. Lauren had already passed her stop a while ago, but had stayed on the bus under the pretence of going to meet a friend. 'I enjoyed talking to you though, let me get your number so we can continue, ennit.'

He reached over, handed her his phone and she eagerly tapped in eleven digits.

'What should I save it as? I bet you've got pure girls in your phone! Probably can't tell who is who...' She giggled, but her ears were pricked for his response.

'Ah, so you think I'm a player, yeah?' Zee smiled.

'Nah, I'm just saying because Lauren ain't the most original name, ennit.'

'Don't worry, I'll remember ya... but will you remember me?' He winked and sloped off the bus.

Lauren was still grinning when the text message popped up on her phone:

Nice 2 meet ya sxy. It's Zee. Inabit.

The quiet of the residential side streets was nothing compared to the silence that swamped Lauren when she reached the main road. At any other time, Soho Road was a bustling artery of the city with buses nosing their way through traffic lined up end to end, and people spilling onto the streets from newsagents, banks, supermarkets and fast food takeaways. Even on a Sunday evening there would be the footfall of worshippers, making their way to and from church services and Sunday dinners. But today the streets were completely deserted, except for the fluorescent jackets of police officers studding the empty road at intervals in either direction, as far as the eye could see. They glowed in the weak October light.

Lauren dug her hands deep into the pockets of her cropped white jacket, wanting to draw the fur-lined hood up and over her ears to ward off an imaginary chill. But, conscious that the action might make her look suspicious, she settled for clenching her fists inside her pockets and kept walking. Each officer she passed mutely watched her go.

As Lauren approached the turn that she needed to take, she glimpsed a small fluorescent cluster outside the blue shutters of the afro hair and beauty shop ahead. *Maybe they were there to collect forensic evidence,* she thought. Maybe a young girl *had* been raped after she was caught shoplifting. It seemed plausible enough: everyone knew someone who had stolen something from a hair shop, that is, if they weren't a thief themselves. Whenever she went into one of the Asian-owned shops on the high street she would be shadowed by one of the shopkeepers as the employees talked over her head in Urdu or Punjabi, or whatever language it was that they spoke. If the young girl *was* assaulted then the fear alone would be reason not to go to the police immediately. Lauren could sympathise with that, but if the girl was here illegally too? Of course she could never report it.

'I heard that she probably didn't report it because she

voluntarily spread her legs,' Melissa had said with authority on the phone the day before. 'She probably got caught teefin' and when they threatened to call the feds she got shook because she's not got papers and offered up the pum-pum! But you know how them men are – what's the word? – *repressed*, ennit, and they think we're easy compared to their women. Their religion only lets them sex their wives to have kids – they ain't allowed to use johnnies or nothing!'

'Ain't that Catholics, though?' Lauren had asked.

'Catholics, Pakistanis, Jehovah's Witnesses, it's all of 'em!'

She hadn't told Melissa about Zee, of course. She could already imagine the look of disgust darkening her face and her reaction – '*Blood!* Are you mad? You wa'an end up chop up in likkle bits when they come for the honour killing?' Or maybe she'd just be shocked that Lauren was talking to a boy, any boy, Asian or not. Melissa often teased her about her inexperience, and when Theo at college had sidled up to her as they waited outside the chip shop, Melissa had cut in: 'You're tryna chat to Lauren?! I'll tell ya now, you'll be disappointed! Her pussy's tighter than a cat's arsehole!' Then she had cackled wildly, savouring the sting of her vulgarity.

Lauren hadn't realised that she'd stopped in the street, staring in the direction of the alleged crime scene until an officer approached.

'Miss, are you lost?'

'N... no, I'm sorry.'

'You best be getting home, not the safest time for a Sunday stroll.'

The officer nodded towards the hair shop, and Lauren quickly turned the corner, not slowing down until she reached the end of Zee's road. She stopped to inspect her reflection in the window of a parked car, rearranging the two braids that snaked out from the nape of her neck. She smoothed down the careful display of fine hairs that radiated from her hairline and tutted to herself for not bringing any Jamm gel to slick down the few wayward kinks. For a second, her mind strayed to the image of a frightened fourteen-year-old in the back storeroom of a hair and beauty shop. She shook the image from her mind and pulled out her phone. She was ready.

Am on ya road xox

Orite. Com 2 numba 46.

She began walking past the terraced houses.

Shud I knock on or w8? xox

Na u can knok. Ma rents av gon out.

Panic flared through Lauren's mind. Did Zee expect her to come in? Everyone knew what a 'free yard' meant, but he'd never even hinted at it on the phone or in any of his text messages. Her stomach fluttered as she approached the door. The brick wall that enclosed the small concrete rectangle in front of No. 46 felt like an omen, but against her better judgement, Lauren announced her arrival with a flap of the black letterbox. The door opened and Zee stood in the crack. He greeted her with a crooked smile, his brown eyes twinkling behind long lashes, and Lauren relaxed instantly.

'You alri–'

'Oi, Zameer, who's that?'

'Nun'ya business!' Zee turned to holler at someone behind him and Lauren could make out a shadowed profile approach before the door was whipped open wider, and a slightly younger boy peered around it, his eyes narrowed.

'Didn't know you was into black bitches, cuz!'

'Shut the fuck up, ya prick!' Zee spat.

'Out in da street, dey call it muuuuurdahh!' The boy's voice cracked as it sang. Zee wrenched the door from his grip and slammed it shut behind him.

After a few brisk paces down the road, he apologised gruffly. Lauren nodded in acknowledgement, but she wanted to ask Zee what the bad impression of Damian Marley was all about. She waited a few moments then decided against it, feeling shyness weighing down her tongue. It was a lot easier to talk for hours by text or under the cover of darkness on the phone, but having Zee right here, striding alongside her in his dark blue Armani jeans and crisp white Nike windbreaker, she was lost for words.

'So where d'ya wanna go?' He finally asked her.

'Erm, I don't mind.'

Zee stopped and surveyed the street.

'Let's go park, ennit.'

He crossed the street without waiting for her and she skipped a little to keep up with him. As they cut through the gullies that ran between the tightly packed red-brick houses, they made small talk, slowly warming to each other's physical presence. Neither of them mentioned the riot, the rumours, or the deserted streets around them. But when they turned onto another main road, Zee's swagger disappeared, stopping Lauren mid-sentence as she followed his hard stare.

Ahead of them was a tight knot of black boys, uniformed in dark clothing with hoods and hats. Their hands were tucked suggestively in the low waistbands of their sagging tracksuit bottoms. Zee regained his posture, setting his jaw with his chin in the air before continuing with an exaggerated lean.

'Come, let's cross the road, it'll be quicker.'

Lauren's stomach turned as they crossed, Zee practically sprinting ahead of her. The cohort of boys turned in silent unison to watch them, before one called out.

'Yo! You got a fag, blood?'

Zee paused before replying but didn't break his stride.

'Nah, blood. I don't smoke, ennit.'

Lauren felt their stares burning holes through her. She heard one of them mutter something to the others and they all cracked into a menacing snicker.

'Where you running to, blood?' Another called out.

Zee drew parallel to them on the opposite side of the road and stopped, turning to face them square on.

'Nowhere, blood. Just got places to go, ennit.'

'Where you going with her, though?'

Zee drew himself taller. Lauren nudged his arm, her heart thundering in her ribcage.

'Come on, Zee, let's just go,' she said in a low voice.

'You like Asian boys, yeah?' One of the group called out to her with a sneer. Zee frowned, his jaw set even tighter.

'Zee, let's *go*.' Lauren's voice trembled.

'You must wanna get fucking raped as well, ya slag!' The sneer bubbled into anger, and he jumped down from his perch on a wall.

'Oi, leave her, blood! If she likes Paki dick, that's her business, ennit,' a voice said, before turning to Lauren. 'We'll remember ya face! Make sure we don't catch ya on road again, or you'll catch a dutty slap!'

He spat on the floor and Lauren pulled Zee away, her hands shaking and tears caught in her lower lashes.

They walked in silence until they reached the empty park. The perimeter was ringed with short evergreen bushes, and as they entered Zee aimed a vicious kick at one, scattering leaves and dirt.

'Fucking pricks! I should have called my cousins down and we'd have fucking battered them!' He spat, before adding under his breath: 'Fucking black dickheads!'

'You what?' Lauren stopped and looked at him.

Zee breathed heavily through his nose. 'Soz, I'm just angry, ennit. Fucking dickheads, man – all of 'em!'

'There's no need to make it about skin colour, though.'

'What d'ya mean?' Zee looked at her. 'They called me a Paki first!'

Lauren took a deep breath, trying to discreetly dab around

her eyes. 'It's probably just the atmosphere, ennit, a lot's happened. I heard a black boy got stabbed and died the other day. Frustrations, ennit.'

'So you don't mind that they said they're gonna slap you?'

'Nah, obviously, but –'

'Listen, it's all lies anyway. We don't do that, that's not our culture.'

'Do what?'

'You know... people are saying a black girl got raped, ennit, I'm saying we don't do that.'

'So you know the man who owns the shop?'

'Nah, I'm just saying, we're not animals like... like other people. The girl probably made it up, they're all liars.'

'Who's *they*?'

'Nah... no, I mean, I don't know, man. All I know is –'

'You people don't do that, I know, I know! So which people *do* do that?' Lauren's tone was confrontational. She could feel the adrenaline still in her system, but the fear had been replaced by the impulse to fight.

'I don't know, fucking... fucking white people, ennit? They're the ones that sold you lot into fucking slavery!'

'Not all black people are slaves, you know.'

'Nah, man, you don't get what I mean – fuck it! Why are we fucking arguing about this shit anyway? Don't make no fucking sense!' Zee sat down heavily on a park bench, but Lauren stayed standing. The ground had shifted beneath her feet.

'What?' Zee lifted his head. 'You wanna go home or something?'

Lauren didn't answer. She could go home, but it would mean a long walk by herself and maybe another run-in with those boys on the corner, or maybe the police would see her doubling back and get suspicious. She had come so far, she had lied to her mother twice already, she might as well stay.

'Just sit down, man, relax. I'm sorry, man, we shouldn't even be talking about this shit. It's got nothing to do with us.'

Lauren slowly sat down next to him. They both stared ahead in silence.

'I don't like this bench,' Zee said after a while. He stood up and held out a hand. 'Let's go by the canal, it's better.' Lauren allowed herself to be pulled to her feet and followed Zee.

Crossing the empty park made Lauren feel like they were soldiers moving across No Man's Land. They walked diagonally across the open green, winding their way behind the empty basketball court, and towards the canal. Lauren didn't relax until Zee had finally settled on a bench near the low bridge where, thankfully, they'd be out of sight.

'You know what messed this whole thing up from the beginning?' Zee asked, his brow furrowed and serious.

Lauren shrugged.

'You didn't give me a hug when you first saw me.'

He let a sly smile creep across his lips. Lauren shook her head, turning away to hide her own grin.

'If you had give me a hug, none of that shit would have happened – I promise ya!'

'Well, it's too late now, it happened,' Lauren mumbled into her collar, but she was still smiling.

Zee stretched out his arms and Lauren feigned reluctance as she leaned into him. He smelled of Joop! Homme and hair wax. After a brief embrace she began to pull away but he locked his arms around her waist and pulled her in closer, so close she could see the spray of dark hairs beginning to form a moustache above his mouth.

'What's that on your lips? It looks nice.'

'Just lipgloss, ennit.'

'What's it taste like?'

Lauren licked her lips. 'I dunno.'

'Let me have a taste.'

Lauren's giggle was silenced as Zee pushed his lips against hers. He held them there briefly, before pulling away.

'What's wrong? Why you so stiff?'

'Nothing, I just… I mean, I –' Lauren stuttered.

'You've never kissed someone before?' A wicked smile played on Zee's lips as he felt her shift in his grip. 'Wait – *how* old are ya?'

Embarrassed, Lauren tried to turn and push him away, but he tightened the lock of his arms and pulled her closer.

'I'm just playing, man, chill out. Just do what I do.'

He kissed her again, and her body relaxed into his. She felt his hands travel from her waist up her back, and slide into the warmth beneath her jacket. A police siren wailed past on the bridge above them and at the same time her phone began to ring buried deep within her bag. It would probably be her mother. Maybe she had called Melissa's house and realised that Lauren wasn't there. If so there would be hell to pay at some point, but right then the only thing that Lauren could think about was how Zee's tongue tasted of peppermint.

Blind Circles

Joel Lane

WHEN A LORRY DRIVER in north central Birmingham takes the wrong fork at Perry Barr, he or she comes upon a lonely and faceless country. The Aldridge Road passes the City Cemetery and bears north-east into a wasteland of garages, factories, scrap yards and expressways. The only sounds are dogs barking and cars backfiring. The roads widen, as if fattened by their diet of oil-soaked rain. The trees fade away and the colour washes out of the skyline, leaving only a blank repeated motif of tarmac, breeze-block and concrete. It's a screensaver of a district.

At a roundabout with more exits than a roundabout ought to have, the driver has a choice of heading west towards Walsall or east towards Sutton Coldfield. A mile either way from the grey factory-farm of the Kings Road estate, a more normal West Midlands landscape begins to assert itself. Stopping for a drink, or even a meal, becomes an idea that one can contemplate without panic. With the slight drop in altitude, the air seems to be a little easier to breathe. Afterwards, the driver may learn that he has been through Kingstanding.

Before things really kicked off there, it had always been a trouble spot. Vicious fights every weekend. Racist attacks, arson, gang murders. Industrial decline has made a mess of north Birmingham in general. But Kingstanding had something else, a vibe of imprisonment that was hard to explain in terms of familiar issues like unemployment and lack of resources. Being at once the highest and the most northern district of Birmingham, it had something to prove. Little gangs of scarred and tattooed Kings Road lads patrolled the district at all times, looking for trouble. They claimed to be enforcing the law, but they'd smash up anyone whose skin, face or attitude didn't suit them. They wore camo gear to make themselves more visible.

In the autumn of 2002, I was sent over to the Kingstanding Circle station to cover for an officer on sick leave. They had two other people ill at the same time, so they'd asked for help. I drove there early on a Sunday morning, and just had time to register the grey vacuum of the area before I had to clock in and start interviewing some of the hard cases they'd kept in overnight. The first one was a lad named Terry. He'd attacked an anti-war stall in the Circle that was set up by four students from UCE. Smashed the stall, broken one of their faces.

Terry was wearing a combat jacket over a 'No Surrender to the IRA' sweat-shirt. He introduced himself as 'Terry McCann, Aryan Defence Militia, National Front, UVF,' and gave a Hitler salute. The Aryan Defence Militia were the gang of losers he hung around with at weekends, patrolling the streets. He was a skinny boy with a pale web of scar tissue across the left side of his face. Seeing him reminded me immediately of the thugs who'd bullied me in secondary school. I wanted to punch him, which didn't help me interview him effectively.

As usual with that type, his remarks were a mixture of scrambled knowledge and pure fantasy. 'We need to police this area. The police are all nigger lovers. The Macpherson Report said they have to be, there's no room for white patriots in the Force. They proved it yesterday, they let those nigger lovers put up a stall here. *Students.* Do they fucking live in Kingstanding? Do they know what we've been through with the Pakis and the niggers and the asylum seekers?'

'And the Jews and the gypsies,' I said. 'Don't forget them.'

'You don't live here, do you?' His face tightened with hatred, became almost childlike, 'I've never seen you here before. What gives you the right to come here and tell us how to behave? What do you know about Kingstanding?'

'I know the law. We're here to uphold the law. It doesn't change from one street to another.'

'There's only one law. That's the law of racial survival.'

I took a deep breath. 'We've got a statement here from one of the lads you attacked yesterday. I want you to read it and tell me if there's anything you disagree with.' Terry nodded. I passed him the statement.

His eyes flickered over the page, without focusing. Suddenly, he spat on it. I snatched it back. 'It's not written in English,' he said flatly. 'It's written in nigger lover language.'

I nodded. 'I'll read it to you, OK?'

'Fuck off. I can fucking read. There's something wrong with my eyes.' He looked at me for a moment, then looked away. I'd taken his bloodshot, unfocused gaze to be the effect of lack of sleep.

I held up a copy of the *Police Gazette*, with a headline about arson. 'What does that say?'

'It says you're a nigger lover.'

'Look son, you're really pissing me off. You're facing two assault charges. If you don't watch out, you'll be looking at six months in prison.'

'Good job I won't be able to see them then, isn't it?'

We took a statement from him, but he needed help to sign it. His friends were waiting for him outside the station; three guys with camo jackets and dogs on long leads. I stood in the doorway, watching as they led him away. He didn't seem able to find his way home alone. The other lads had scars worse than his, and one had 'NF' tattooed on the back of his head.

By the end of the week, the Kingstanding station was still three officers down. I was needed back at Acocks Green, so they arranged for more cover. The three sick officers were all men. It hadn't occurred to me to ask what was wrong with them.

It was over the winter that things really began to change. I kept in touch with DC Bestwick at the Kingstanding station, who was bewildered by the situation. 'Some kind of epidemic. All these guys slowly going blind. Maybe it's an infection carried by dogs. I swear they're using their guard dogs as guide dogs.' Within three months, several dozen cases of blindness were reported. Mostly among violent lads who were known to the police. They were still drinking and fighting, guided by their mates, but at least they weren't patrolling the streets any more.

There was something else, too. Kingstanding wasn't the kind of district where strangers were allowed to breathe easily. In fact, they weren't allowed to breathe at all. But several newcomers had been spotted among the Kings Road estate crowd, blending in as if they'd always belonged there. In fact, Bestwick said, they were as popular as if they'd just come out of Borstal. 'There's four or five of the bastards. Dunno where they've come from. Male, white, fair-haired. I mean *really* white. Albino, maybe. Always surrounded by a gang of Kings Road hard cases who are buying them drinks and fucking cigarettes. Maybe they're the Ku Klux Klan.'

That wasn't as facetious a remark as it might sound. Bestwick was from near Manchester, where the BNP were starting to burn holes in the map. I'd always thought the fascists were a threat at a personal level, unable to affect things on any bigger scale; but Oldham and Burnley had shown that the BNP were capable of taking over a town, once their *agent provocateur* tactics had set communities at each other's throats.

In October, fifty NF supporters had marched through Kingstanding. And where they went, the boot boys and the arsonists were bound to follow.

In January, I drove up there while off duty. Traces of frost glimmered on the pavements like slug trails. Half the shops in Kingstanding Circle were boarded up. I waited for twenty minutes, then saw two guys coming over the hill from the cemetery. They were wearing combat jackets and dark glasses. They both had Alsatians on leads. Were they blind, or did they just feel like walking slowly? No doubt they'd trod the same street every day of their lives. Something Bestwick had said came back to me. 'Kingstanding people always say, if you don't live here you can't understand. I always thought that was bullshit. But it's true now. They've made it true. If you don't live here, there's no way you can understand what's happening.'

I waited to see one of the pale newcomers, but none of them came. Every couple of minutes, an HGV or fuel tanker heading out of Birmingham made the road vibrate and the surviving plate-glass windows tremble. A sign above one of the boarded-up shops said *WINDOW BLINDS*. I thought, *How do you make a window blind? Turn away from it.* My hand turned the key in the ignition, and five minutes later I was out of there.

Five weeks later, I was back. It was night, and from the Kingstanding Road I could see the city's lights spread for miles ahead of me: Newtown, Aston, the city centre. This district was a crow's nest, a vantage point for anyone who wanted to watch over the city. It was still midwinter here: the ground was tacky with frost, and the air was thin and sharp. Through the layers of traffic noise, I could hear dogs barking.

There was some kind of political meeting going on tomorrow night. Bestwick hadn't been sure of the details, but it was a fairly safe bet that it wasn't the SWP. There'd been no leaflets or posters, but everyone seemed to know about it. Some movement calling itself Light of the North – Bestwick was sure it had to do with the blond strangers. 'North as in Nordic, Aryan. Maybe they're a heavy metal band.' And maybe not. The meeting was at a local primary school.

I parked my car by King's Standing Wood. No wonder they had masculinity issues around here. The trees were grey and angular in the moonlight, like girders in some vast warehouse. There was no one on the streets. I let myself into the caretaker's office at the back of the school. This had taken some persuasion, but the caretaker had a cottaging history that he didn't want the school to know about. At night all cats are grey.

Through a gap in the blinds, I surveyed the school car park and the street beyond it. The window was just open. There was a smell of burning, not fresh; maybe the remnants of a November bonfire. The flickering of car lights in the distance was the only movement. And then, around midnight, I saw one of them. A pale man with hair like frost. He was wearing a thin denim jacket, but didn't appear to be cold. He glanced around the car park, then looked at the school. Quickly, I stepped away from the window. When I looked out again, he was walking calmly away in the direction of Kingstanding Circle.

After that, it happened every hour. They were clearly patrolling, or at least watching the streets. As far as I could tell, there was no one else around. Not even a stray cat. The white men – and Bestwick was right, they were probably albino – had a kind of blank, restless purpose about them. Like they had passports to the night. Their cold wakefulness got into my head and overcame any thoughts of sleep. I could see why they might have a following in this place. Somehow, they embodied the idea of surveillance. I had a confused sense of territories shifting, a different world being mapped out around me.

Some time between three and four, I heard the first unexpected sound of the night. A scratching at the door, and a faint whimpering caught somewhere between the need to be heard and the need to remain silent. I couldn't see anyone or anything through the window. Tensing myself to be ready for trouble, I opened the door an inch. Nothing. A few inches more. A slanted face poked into the gap. A dog. I let it in and it stood on the doormat, shivering. An idea took shape in my sleep-deprived brain. The dog could be my disguise. What else were dogs for?

The moon was a fraction short of its profile the night before. The sounds of distant traffic permeated the stillness, like nocturnal voices in a tenement house. As far as I could judge, the crowd gathering in the school car park consisted entirely of blind men and their dogs. Some had walking-sticks and dark glasses; others just gazed blankly around, waiting to be tugged or guided. Nobody spoke. I waited between two cars, with the dog crouched tense at my feet. The glasses turned every face to a sepia photograph. A wedding party from an old family album. They couldn't see me, but I hoped their dogs wouldn't betray me as a stranger.

The school door opened, and one of the pale men came out. The first one I'd seen the night before. 'Leave the dogs here,' he said. There was a trace of something Baltic or Scandinavian in his voice. 'Just leave them. Come inside.' One by one, the blind men dropped their leads. The dogs stayed where they were, trembling from cold or tension. Their owners shuffled towards the open doorway. Two of the white men caught their arms, guided them calmly into the school.

I shut my eyes as I approached them, so they wouldn't realise I could see. The hand that gripped my coat sleeve felt as light and hard as bone. I tripped on the doorstep and almost fell. The interior of the school was as stark as the exterior: no paintings or photographs, no signs of children's presence. I wondered if it had closed down. There were a few more of the blond men waiting inside. About seven in all. I couldn't tell them apart, but that was the dark glasses limiting my sight. And I had to be careful not to look directly at anyone.

Chairs had been set up in tidy rows to occupy the school hall, as if for a parents' meeting. I thought momentarily that my own junior school had been built on a much larger scale. I'd thought the same thing when I first took my daughter Julia to school in Acocks Green. Nearly fifteen years before. We're never ready for change, but we get used to it, and then we're not ready for things staying the same.

It took a while to get everyone seated. I wondered why we all had to face the same way, when none of us could see. Order? Three of the newcomers sat at the front, behind a small table. Evidently they took 'right of assembly' literally around here. One of them rapped on the table. 'Good evening. We are here tonight for one reason. *Law* and *order.*' His thin voice cut through the silence of the hall. He made the words sound like the names of unfamiliar deities. 'Not the bogus law and order of the Government and the police. We all know whose agenda they serve. We stand for true law and order. The law of our race. The order of nature. Day and night, winter and summer, man and beast. We are the truth. And you are the army.'

I half expected the audience to respond with a co-ordinated Nazi salute. But they sat there like crop-haired statues, waiting for the next word. The speaker stood up. He was very thin, I noticed. The glasses meant I couldn't see his eyes properly. For some reason. I was glad of that. 'Kingstanding used to be a white area,' he said. 'Britain used to be a white country. And they will be again. Together we will cut out the tumours of corruption and deceit. The doctrine of racial equality and the cancer of race mixing. The Jewish lies and the poison of Islam.

We will cut them out. We will burn them out.' The most disturbing thing was his total calmness, and the lack of any reaction on the part of the audience. How had they come so far from the human world? Bestwick was right: I didn't understand.

The other two men behind the table stood up. 'Are you with us?' one of them said. 'Or are you with the appeasers and the liberals and the bureaucrats who've sold out your heritage? Are you with the shit at the bottom of the multiracial swamp? Or are you rising into the Light of the North?'

The response came: 'Light of the North!' Some fifty voices, all bellowing at once. I shouted with them, so as not to be suspected; but the words came easily, and I wondered how many fascists started by just trying to blend in. 'Light of the North!' we repeated, and the old walls echoed the vowels. A few of the dogs outside began to bark.

The pale man who'd not yet spoken put his hands to his face and breathed on them, as if trying to thaw them out. When he opened his hands, something was glowing between them. A thin flame, dead white, like a burning strip of mercury in a school chemistry lesson. I forced myself not to look at it. I wasn't supposed to see anything.

'Come forth to receive the Light,' he said. 'One at a time. Wait to be taken forth. Wait… and see.' The shimmering flame obscured his face. The other two men came down to the front row of chairs. Each of them took a blind man by the arm and led him towards the colourless fire. More of the dogs were barking now, and I could hear a faint scratching at the door.

As the first of the believers approached the flame, his face seemed to lose all expression. The stranger's white hand drained it of features. When the flame moved away, the face was a blank mass of scar tissue, like an unfinished doll. The believer fell away to one side of the stage. His body made no sound when it hit the floor. The stranger's hands danced in the air, and the flame between them was so bright I couldn't have looked at it without dark glasses. The second believer approached the stage, one hand feeling the air in front of him.

The blind men continued to respond to the strangers' touch, rising two by two to the stage and the white flame. The limp bodies piled up on either side. I tried not to see too much, but my eyes refused to close. I was sitting near the edge of the third row. How long before I was grabbed and taken to the starving light? And what would they do to me if I resisted? The worst thing was that I didn't want to resist.

The only sound I could hear was the barking of the dogs outside. It was getting louder, but it didn't seem relevant. They were thumping against the door now, their soft mindless bodies unable to breach the security of the building. We'd deal with them, and everyone, later. For now, the only reality was the white flame and the scar of its light. The power, the need. Two more believers were taken and drained, their form released into the light, their husks dropped. Then two more. I could smell burning, but it wasn't like any burning I had smelt before. The air in the hall was as cold as ice.

Something hit the outside of a window to my right. And again. Glass splintered. The barking was suddenly much louder. More glass fell inwards, and dogs poured through the gap. I could see their breath white in the air.

As more dogs leapt in behind them, they attacked the holder of the flame. He fell, the pure light in his hands becoming a prism of twisted colours. The dogs tore at him. The other pale men backed off, panicking. The territories were changing again. I reached up to my face and slipped off the glasses. What the dogs on the stage were ripping apart had no blood. He was white all the way through.

Another window broke, and more dogs came in. Every dog in Kingstanding must have been outside the school that night. One by one, the strangers were torn to colourless shreds. The dogs didn't eat whatever passed for their flesh: they killed and moved on. The blind men – those still alive – were on their feet, calling out to each other or their dogs, trying to make sense of this chaos where everything had been so simple. The floor was littered with broken glass.

I didn't want to stay. I didn't want to help the survivors or clean up the mess. Above all, I didn't want to look at the featureless waxy blobs that had been human faces, the inert bodies scattered around the stage like props. I walked out into the hallway, found the bolt on the school door and slipped it free. Leaving the door open, I walked back to my car. The streets were empty. Apart from the traffic, of course.

My car was still where I had left it, on the edge of King's Standing Wood. The moon was clouded over, but the accumulated light of cars and buildings hung over the trees and made their branches just visible against the bare ground. I got into the car and fumbled with the ignition key. My hands were shaking too badly for me to drive. A streetlamp showed me my own face in the rear-view mirror. I watched the reflection of my breath clouding the still air. After a while, the interior of the car warmed up a little and my breath was clear. I sat there, not moving, until dawn began to creep through the trees. Then I started the engine and drove home.

A Game of Chess

Malachi McIntosh

i. The Set-Up

All of this happened at a strange time in my life. My wife and I were going through a rough patch, in part because I'd just walked away from what seemed like a dream job as a manager at a charity in the Black Country – a job that, on paper, was perfect – an exact match for my interests and experience – but in practice was pretty awful; the whole thing overseen by a director that, as hard as I'd tried, I couldn't ever see eye-to-eye with, on anything.

So I left it. Was unemployed for the first time since age fifteen and drifting – literally, figuratively – my wife under a lot of pressure to support us both.

We weren't young then, my wife and I, still aren't now. We were rounding out the edge of our thirties and childless, with all the social pressures and concerns that that raises: the wrinkled brows from friends who say it took them ages too, my in-laws talking loudly, and always, about my wife's nieces and nephews, and my wife's own worries about time.

And it was strange – all strange – a weird moment in both our lives, and then seeing my father made it worse.

★

Let me explain. I'd spent almost my entire life working. I'd done everything you can think of – from menial jobs at school-age through to every post you can hold in an office, dabbled in teaching, even completed an internship in advertising. I'd always worked, defined myself by working, and losing that job made me feel like I'd lost myself – the feeling even worse because leaving was something I'd chosen.

It wasn't the first time I'd left something, of course, but before there had always been another opportunity, some new challenge lined up, something else waiting. My hope after leaving was to jump straight into a new role but there wasn't any direct match for me in the city and then I woke up one day and just felt hollow. And so, when my wife left in the mornings, instead of searching for vacancies like I told her I was, I spent whole days lying idle, up to absolutely nothing, sometimes only showering an hour before she came home.

When I did leave the house I was just idleness in motion. And I wandered, mostly along the canals down toward the Jewellery Quarter, or the opposite way out to Selly Oak and the university, or over into town. Any of those three routes or along the slowly more overgrown towpaths toward Sandwell, following, when I did, like I was homing, a path that took me close to where I used to work and into the dream of how my job would've been if I'd kept it, should've been if it was right for me.

I could cut whole chunks out of days that way, by wandering, wandering and thinking and feeling frustrated hope, no motivation, deep in the questioning that had become more intense as I'd grown older about what I was doing, where I was going.

I wasn't unhappy. I should say that now: I wasn't unhappy. But I wandered. Never alone, totally; even the secluded areas of the canals had passers-by; there were always, are always, other people, wandering in some ways too, I suppose, most with an obvious reason – out shopping on days off; mothers with their children; tourists, who I always questioned (who would come as a tourist to *Birmingham*?); school skivers of all types, sans blazers, ties hidden or flapping proud.

On the days I took the main streets they were always crowded and I'd watch the mothers – the posh ones with their all-terrain pushchairs in cafés, others with old-style quickfolds – their kids sitting and looking listless, half-drugged, a lot of women around the Bullring with more children than made sense, some too young.

I'd never aspired to be a stereotype, a breadwinner or whatever, but I was starting to feel like I'd turned into one of the men I'd wished I'd never be – wreckage, unmotivated and aimless – and felt shame for thinking that as I thought it; felt shame for the guilt of association; felt shame that I wasn't at home fixing my CV, or on Guardian Jobs, or emailing contacts; felt shame that I was wallowing and feeling sorry for myself about something I'd chosen that others had no choice but to choose, and walked and wandered and felt idle, and one day – out of our flat, into the canals, through the ICC, up the stairs and past all the endless construction by the library, round the barriers thrown up for even more building work by Victoria Square – I saw my father.

★

My response was instant, quick, a reflex so automatic it almost scared me: I flinched and ducked, convulsed my whole body back behind some hoardings to hide myself so he couldn't see me. To describe what I saw, the way that he looked, from my hiding place, makes my panic even more ridiculous. But what matters isn't really what he looked like, it was what he was doing, the simple fact that he was there. In outline: an old black man, well past middle age, in a council jumpsuit, wheeling a small wheelie bin with brooms and a dustpan clipped onto it and picking up rubbish. I'm not sure what somebody else would have seen, if they would have even seen him, but for me, there he was, my own father, gathering trash.

★

That night I cooked dinner for my wife. It was my responsibility in theory. We'd agreed that since I was the one at home all day with free time, that I would be the one to make meals for us and keep the house clean. The fact was, though, that it was something I'd been doing less and less. But that night I did it properly, fully – I went to the shops, bought ingredients, chopped and boiled and fried a recipe from a cookbook, spent near to ninety minutes making and mixing before she came home to a laid table, wine, all of it, her usual sigh and clash of keys at the door, the tumble of her kicked shoes followed by her face – surprise.

There was no occasion, I said. It was just recognition that I needed to step things up, snap out of my funk. She was tentative at first, knew how I'd been feeling, asked to help and I said, Of course not, no, pulled her seat out and asked her about her day, my mind wholly and totally, fully and completely in that moment when I saw my father so that, later, after the wine, in bed, I had to apologise. I was really sorry. I was really tired.

ii. Bishop's Pawn to F3

My first few times to the square I went just to verify, my image of his face for so long a mixture of the last few pictures he took with me: an adult man standing next to a child in various places, a child whose own features hadn't yet crystallised into mine.

It took a few visits to understand his routine. He didn't come through every day, seemed to just work every other. He arrived at the square at about ten and was gone within twenty minutes, meticulous, the broom and pan used on every object on the ground, plastic and cans from bushes collected with another tool.

I found a café where I could sit so he couldn't see me, ordered filtered coffee and watched him from when he arrived until he left. Gradually, over a week, I started to see all the parts of me that were his: the stockiness of his midriff, his height, the pattern of baldness on his head foreshadowing mine, the wrinkles above his eyebrows piling as he went. The work itself was endless – a job that could never be done – even as he collected crisp packets and bottles, people dropped them around him. But he still worked, steady, getting almost everything, then moved on.

*

At home I was distracted. I slacked off more and more, stopped cleaning, let the dishes I made in the morning fester in the sink, stopped washing clothes, left half-browsed magazines and newspapers open everywhere, charger cables snaking unconnected across floors, surfaces.

My wife and I had the conversation we were bound to have at some stage, after she probed around to find out about the successfulness, or not, of my job search.

I said there wasn't anything much suitable I could see and she said, her face tightening, It's fine, we had time, we could go on a bit longer on one income, and I responded to something that may or may not have been implied.

I am trying.

I know, she said, added that she could do more around the house as well, said it wasn't fair it was all on me.

It's fair. It's fine. I don't have a job.

You've got a job, she said. Your job is to get a job.

★

And so the next week. Back to the square and a man I hadn't seen in thirty years. In the middle of a city I hadn't lived in since I was a child. Back to the streets and people and walking and nothing else. My father working while I watched.

iii. Queen's Pawn to E5

My last clear memory before seeing him there was a lesson that he taught me. My mother and I had just moved from Birmingham to London, or hadn't been in London long, when she sent me back to stay with him.

I remember we travelled by train, but I don't remember them exchanging any words, and can't remember now where my mother went, only that she met me at the station at the end of the week. There are other things: the smell of the old Bullring, the reeking meat of halved, quartered and hanging animals at the market, and what, I think, but don't know now for sure, was sawdust on the ground. It was the summer holidays, so it was warm, the whole city, to me, both more cramped and more spacious than the London I was coming to know. I remember swings, trees, parks, my father driving us to the living rooms of his friends and family until his car broke down. All that and a game of chess. I was eight years old.

★

From the car or the bus into the houses of old Jamaicans. I ate plates piled with domes of food, met what must have been my father's girlfriend and noticed – I think I noticed – that she was very young.

He had a strict routine. Every morning I was with him he'd boil three eggs, two for himself, set toast then play a tape, in my memory only ever Bobby Brown — *everybody's talking/ all this stuff about me/why don't they just let me live* — and he'd do calisthenics — sit-ups, push-ups, planks where he'd jump his feet in and out between his arms. I watched him and thought he was some kind of superhero, tried to copy him and failed, and that only made him more like a god.

After his exercises we'd go visiting, but this day — and I don't remember what day it was — he said we'd play chess.

I didn't know the game. Or I knew of it but that was all. He showed me the basics on a blank board: first each piece and how it moved, then how to set up the sides, then that you usually start with white but don't have to, then that the goal was to capture the king.

We played, his hands steepled underneath his chin as he went, his head to the side and eyes at mine when I reached to move each piece. He coached me: Are you sure? What about that one there, how does it move? Look there. Be careful. Always think about how I could take you.

I don't know what self-control it took for him not to just swat me aside, to make me feel like I had a chance. It's always escaped me — I always make things too easy in games with children, make it obvious that I'm holding back, which they can sometimes see, resent. But he, my father, made it feel balanced and equal, until the end.

Across his whole introduction of chess to me, he never explained how you win, that the goal is to immobilise the king, paralyse him in place without an escape, not to slide ahead your attacking pieces and get him off the board. He didn't tell me about check or checkmate, only said, Look, I'll take your queen unless she moves, or Watch yourself. He never told me that the game wasn't about brute force, it was won with patience, subtlety.

So at the end, with most of my pieces lost, but a fair few of his in my hands, he trapped me. He didn't say anything. I tried to move to break free but he touched my shoulder.

What about him? he pointed.

I tried again.

What about him? He pointed. You're not thinking about him.

I set the king down and studied the board. Find a way out, he said.

I studied and studied, glanced up at him, steepled my hands under my chin like he did, thinking maybe it was some way to trigger better thoughts. I shook my head, stubborn, and studied. He told me to take a break and bathe, and afterwards, in clean clothes and still damp, I was straight back to the board.

We left for another day of me shadowing him with the pieces still in place. This time I followed him to a series of odd jobs that he did – minor repairs, plumbing, electrics – and when we came back, late, I sat and studied, steepled my hands and studied and he didn't tell me why I was stuck until the next morning.

iv. Knight's Pawn to G4

I didn't see him again after that. He and the girlfriend moved away, my mother thought. My mother found someone else, for a time. My father called on birthdays for years, then stopped. Then I was a teenager and didn't care. More or less.

But always when I visited other cities I'd wonder if a face I glimpsed was his. I'd sometimes go to work meetings or travel and see an older commuter or supervisor and think, *Is that him?* But it was never him, because it couldn't be. He wouldn't have those jobs, or be moving through those spaces. Those possibilities were so remote they were close to impossible.

And now he was here, in Birmingham, in the square, and I felt ridiculous watching him. I needed to sort out some sort of plan. I couldn't keep spying on him in secret from a hiding place, pass the rest of my time in memories, then rush home to change and lie to my wife that, No, none of the jobs I'd applied for had replied.

I needed a plan, started to watch critically, tried to think my way through the situation. I paid more attention to people in the square, to the constant traffic of bodies, all the rubbish dropped after he was gone, tossed while he was working. I tried to come up with some meaning for it, the random encounter, the fact that my wife and I had moved to Birmingham only for me to find my father within months of our return. I thought about how small the city was, thought about all the kids I saw – the toddlers, babies, and older ones – the old and modern mix of architecture, the ongoing construction, the city in a cycle of rebirthing itself, the fact that the things that had been here when I came up to see my father three decades ago were now mostly gone, bulldozed to make way for something else, unfinished, tried to link all of that back to myself.

I worked to re-confirm: Was it him? Of course it was. How could I be sure? Because in all ways he was like me, only aged. And he was methodical, and focused, like he had always been, missed nothing.

I knew I had to make contact, but didn't know what to say. Was he alone now like my mother was? Did he think of me? Did he have other kids? The longer I left it, the more I felt like talking to him would be the key that would unlock my life, get me out of the hole I was in, fix things.

v. Break

I wonder if I should have started here instead. With the facts. With an overview:

1.) I was born in the early eighties, in Birmingham

2.) My parents were never married

3.) They split

4.) My mother and I moved to London

5.) We had a good life without him. She did well and so did I. I went to university. Later, I met a girl from Birmingham, who wanted to go back to Birmingham, start a family.

6) I got married. We moved back. I got a new job straight away. Hated it. Quit.

vi. Checkmate

I composed a script:

Hi it's —

I just —

I saw —

I'd pretend that I'd just bumped into him. I'd say I still had the job I'd left. Yes, I had a wife now. Yes, she was fine, great actually, successful. Yes, we were planning to have kids. I didn't think it then but I know now that each sentence was a hand reached down, a piece picked up, another area of the board occupied. As I planned I predicted his responses, tried to outthink him, outflank him. To prove what? To do what? For what? I don't know.

★

I wore a suit on the day, followed my normal route: from our flat along the canal, up through the ICC, up the stairs, out and past the endless construction by the library, into Victoria Square. I took my seat at the café and ordered a black coffee, had a newspaper and unfolded it open on the table, but couldn't stop my hands from shaking.

Opening gambit: eyes over the paper, then widened in feigned shock; body up from the table fast but not too fast, my hand covering my mouth and then a confident smile. And then I'd say:

'Dad it's me.'

'M—' he'd say and turn.

I got up, moved closer, walking toward him.

'Alright?' I'd say casually, grin. 'What are you doing here?'

And then he'd check his tools, the bin, himself, and frown and shake his head, kiss his teeth, wipe his head and say, '*Boy*, you know –'

I was almost next to him, an arms-length away, the imagined conversation vanished and his body hunched, sweeping.

Around us the whole square swarmed with people – all the people who day by day I moved past, wandering their own routes – and I said Hello? and realised my mistake.

When the man turned, this close up, it was obvious. He wasn't my father.

His nose was wrong, the slope of his eyebrows too steep, his hands too wide and his fingers worn – in all the small details, even in the nature of his stare, his thinness, everything – it was all too soft, too weak, all wrong.

But he said my name.

I stood frozen – wholly and completely frozen, stood there longer than I can explain with nothing to say. This man was a stranger, a total stranger. He wasn't my father, couldn't be, but he said my name, and his voice was the voice that I knew, remembered, and I heard: Look again. You're not thinking about him. And if you move there – you see? I can take you.

The Call

Sibyl Ruth

JULIE HAD BEEN IN the room for two and a half hours. She stared out of the window, which looked onto the window of another office.

It had been a quiet shift. One of the regulars wanting to talk about her new cat. A woman who had been referred by her GP for counselling. And somebody wanting information leaflets. Julie had put the contact details for the last two into the file. Neither of them lived anywhere near Oakford Road.

The Project was not like she had imagined in the beginning. Julie had thought that the phone would ring all the time. Women asking, 'Help, what can I do?' immediately after the event. Instead there were long stretches when nobody rang at all. And men rang up wanting support – more of them than Julie had thought possible.

She turned over a page of the newspaper to check the listings. Straightaway she came face-to-face with a smiling photo of Bridget, who was on TV again tonight. Julie tried to decide if the image had been digitally altered or if her old housemate had gone for cosmetic surgery. Maybe it was just an old picture.

With some people you wondered what happened to them. You might do fruitless searches online. In Bridget's case there was no need. It was no great surprise that she'd made a name for herself. The woman had always been single-minded.

Julie reminded herself that she too had been successful in her own way. And would be still if it wasn't for partners who got offered the job they'd always dreamed of. (Just not in London.) Who went on and on until you found yourself agreeing to go with them. Julie had taken a post in a small firm in the Black Country. She told herself it was not a backwards move, but a sideways one. After three months the small firm had amalgamated with a larger company, leaving her without a position of any kind.

Sometimes Julie thought she should have seen it coming. But however good you were, however experienced, there was always a risk you'd get shafted.

Volunteering at the helpline was a way to fill time. And Julie was good at it. She knew how to sound empathic, so people would talk. She understood the need for boundaries.

The phone was ringing. Before she took the call Julie checked her watch. Only a quarter of an hour to the end of her shift.

'Survival Project. Can I help you?'

She filled in the record sheet automatically. Subject of call. Duration. Ethnicity of caller (if known). Then Julie replayed parts of the conversation. Everything she had said.

Hello?

Yes. I'm listening.

You sound very upset...

That's when the girl had begun speaking, so fast the actual words hadn't been easy to catch. Julie had done her best to follow.

So there was a group of you at first?

Not exactly a friend. Just a guy you knew...

And (this would have been last thing): *It's very common for people to blame themselves.*

Somebody was standing over her. It was Naz, the manager.

'We thought you'd gone.'

Julie pushed her chair back.

'I was about to –'

'Are you alright?'

'It was this girl...Woman. She put the phone down.'

Naz reminded Julie sometimes people would ring several times before they could summon up courage to talk.

'No, this one talked. Said she was a student. And she was telling me about what happened. But then she hung up.'

'Maybe there's something you want to discuss?'

Julie hesitated. Chris was away so there was no hurry to get back. Then she remembered how people used to come to her with difficult cases. And now, with Naz, it was the other way around.

She began clearing her things off the desk, and Bridget's picture grinned up at her.

'I'm okay, thanks.'

In London, if Julie didn't feel like going home she walked by the Thames. This city had no proper river.

She'd cross one or other of the bridges. But here the only bridges were over the ring road.

She'd have sat on a bench in one of the squares. There were no beautiful Georgian squares in the middle of Birmingham.

So many reasons not to come back. But Chris kept saying the city had changed. Julie agreed to move because sometimes it was politic to concede. Then, when Chris got keen on a house in the vicinity of Oakford Road, Julie had felt able to put her foot down.

'Out of the question,' she'd said. 'It's a rough area,' and Chris, who didn't really know about Birmingham, had believed her.

Julie was still replaying the phone call as she waited by Moor Street. The overhead display promised a bus would appear soon.

It was all my fault. That's what the girl had said. If only she'd managed to get a name, a few more details. Anything to give Julie a sense of who the girl was, where she might be.

For years Julie had believed the incident with Paul was her fault. She had made mistakes, behaved like a complete idiot. Although, it couldn't ever have happened without Bridget.

At some point the display had been rewritten. The bus must have gone into reverse because now it wouldn't come for ten minutes. It was raining and there were more people in the queue. Meanwhile a stream of wrong buses was scooping up passengers from the nearby shelter, where nobody had to wait.

Julie took another look at the newspaper. She had folded it with Bridget's picture on top.

She would be prepared to bet that Bridget never stood in bus queues. Bridget would take taxis. On the train, Bridget would go first class, taking full advantage of the complimentary tea and coffee.

That man who was too big for his suit – ahead of her in the line – was staring at her again. He'd been doing this off and on, even though Julie was sure she didn't know him.

At times she has wondered if Paul could still be in Birmingham. They might have gone to the same film screening, bought drinks in the same crowded bar. Or even sat at nearby tables, without having the least suspicion. For twenty years, Julie has had her hair cut short. Paul could have put on weight or shaved his moustache off. He could have gone grey or bald.

The staring man gave her the creeps. Plus everybody had begun squashing together because of the rain and Julie hated it when people got too close. She went and stood out on the pavement, then – after getting jostled by passers-by – to the relative space of the next shelter.

Another empty bus pulled up in front of her, opening its

doors with a hiss. Julie stepped back, right into some bloke who said, 'Do you mind?'

So to get away from him – and everybody else – she got on board.

Julie had meant to press the bell after just a couple of stops. But instead she went on sitting there and didn't get out until the university. She thought of it as 'The University', even though in recent years the city had acquired several more of them. But this one was still the biggest.

Over the road young people were streaming in and out of the massive gates. Maybe the girl who'd rung her was amongst them.

Walking on further, Julie realised the main street was different. There were still a few pubs, but the butcher's and the baker's had disappeared. Now it was all mini-markets and takeaways. *Chicken.com. Tasty Pastry.* Only everything was the same underneath. You only had to glance above the shop fronts, up at the grimy brickwork.

Of course, she had been along here in the car. Avoiding this street was next to impossible. But as a driver you only see what's in front of your nose.

Oakford Road was really very close. Having come this far she might as well pay the place a visit.

Julie was not sure why she'd gone to live there.

She'd hardly known Bridget during the first year – apart from lending her pens and letting her borrow the occasional essay. So she had been surprised when the woman suggested a house share. Flattered too. Because even then Bridget had been the sort of person everyone talked about.

Only once they'd moved in had Bridget's strategy become clear. It was the same reason she had got Dan, the shy biochemist, to take the third bedroom. Bridget reckoned neither of them would be any trouble.

As Julie turned off the main road there was a gust of wind. She tightened her grip on the newspaper.

Bridget had never anticipated that she and Dan might become allies who would challenge Bridget about not washing up, not cleaning, never having her cheque book when there was a bill to be paid.

Except it was impossible to make her do stuff she didn't want to do – Bridget just switched tactics. She was in the house less and less. Often she'd only drop by for as long as it took to scoop up an armful of clothes.

Mostly that was a relief. Except – this being long before mobiles – blokes would keep calling round to see her.

Having turned another corner, Julie went back to read the street sign. Yes, it was Oakford Road. It was as if she'd hung on to the knowledge, stashing it away.

At No. 12, a man was letting himself in. Julie could glimpse a rug, the edge of a coffee table. All the houses had doors which opened straight into the living room.

Why did it never occur to her to blame the architects, the builders, who put up these terraces? So little had changed: landlords were still hungry for profit, eager to pack in tenants. When Julie had answered the door to Paul that night, he immediately stepped inside.

'I've come for Bridget.'

'She isn't here at the moment.'

'Okay, I'll wait.'

Paul laid his motorbike helmet down on the chair. He wasn't wearing a leather jacket or a denim one, but some hairy ethnic garment. Julie reckoned he looked a bit odd. But there was no accounting for Bridget's tastes. She felt sorry for the men sometimes.

'Would you like a coffee? While you're waiting.'

He followed her into the kitchen, and – because Julie was in the middle of making toast – she gave him a piece of that as well.

They'd sat in the front room. Dan must have been at the library.

Julie wasn't in the mood for small talk. Fortunately, the silence – apart from the crunch of toast – didn't seem to bother Paul. All the same she got up and pressed play on the tape-machine, without even checking the cassette. (It was Bob Marley.)

After a couple of tracks she said, 'I don't think Bridget's going to show up.'

Paul said it was cool. He added. 'How about a smoke? In exchange for the toast.'

'That's kind – but there's no need.'

Only he'd already got a Golden Virginia tin out of his weird jacket, and was starting to roll a joint.

After a minute he handed it across.

'Thanks.'

The cardboard was damp where his lips had been. Julie took a quick drag, then attempted to pass it back.

'No,' he said. 'That's good stuff. You have to inhale properly.'

He came and sat next to her on the sofa.

'That's better. Yes.'

And Bob Marley played on: *Movement of jah people.*

'You know,' said Paul after the joint was finished. 'Perhaps no one's told you. But you're a lot more attractive than Bridget.'

She tried inching away, but the sofa was too saggy. It was a useless sofa.

'Bridge the Fridge is what some people call her... Frigid Bridget.'

Julie did laugh at that. All the same she was puzzled. Surely Paul must like Bridget – or else he wouldn't have come to see her.

'Why...?'

Except she never finished the question. That's when he'd slid an arm round, pulling her close.

Julie stopped. The house was there all right. But which one was it? Not 104, because the door was at the wrong side. It would either be 102 or 106. Julie tried peering into one window, then the other. That didn't help. They'd got nets up at 102 and 106 had a bunch of artificial flowers, blocking the view. How could she have forgotten the house number, when she remembered so many other things?

At first she quite liked kissing Paul.

There was a feeling of triumph – she was getting one up on Bridget. And it was a new experience. Julie was positive she'd never kissed anyone with a moustache. Not properly.

It was only when he started tugging at her jeans, that it stopped being fun.

'I don't want that.'

Paul told her she was gorgeous. Sexy.

'You can't... No.'

Julie kept thinking Bridget could pick that moment to walk in. How would she react to seeing her with Paul? She might reckon it was funny. She might lose her temper. It was even possible her housemate might want to join in. Or Dan could be outside, fumbling for his key. Julie could see him backing off, shutting the door softly, as he wondered what was wrong with the women he lived with.

Living here was already bad enough. To be found like this would be the absolute end. And no, she wasn't going to suggest to some dodgy mate of Bridget's that they go upstairs.

Julie tried shifting Paul, who had moved his weight onto her. He was taller, but it should have worked. Except the dope was making her floppy, not as strong as usual.

102 looked more likely to be the house, though that could be because the exterior was shabby, with peeling paint. Whereas the owners of 106 had got themselves shiny new uPVC windows.

No. 102 had a low wall. Julie sat on it.

It was possible the girl on the phone lived on one of these streets.

What would she be doing now? Did she intend to talk to anybody apart from Julie? Someone from the Students' Union maybe – like the women's officer. Did they even have women's officers anymore? Julie hoped they did.

'Just relax.' That's what he'd said.

Paul wasn't rough. It didn't hurt when he began to move inside her. What upset Julie was the feeling she had not made herself clear. She hadn't used the right words or behaved in the right way. Because if she had done, then Paul would have got the message.

Relaxing was not a choice, but she did lie still. That meant it would be done sooner. Her guess was that Paul wasn't planning to stick around for long.

This turned out to be correct.

Julie was still trying to do her buttons up while he was retrieving his bike helmet, saying how he had to be getting along.

Somebody had come out of 102 with a crate of rubbish. A woman with purple hair and a tattooed neck, glaring at Julie – in her smart jacket – as if she was a suspicious character.

'Can I help you?'

Julie scrambled to her feet. Was it possible to say this house, or the one two doors down, was where she got raped?

'I've been trying to work out where I am.'

'You're lost?'

'Yes. I was looking for... for Bampton Street.'

Julie stared at the crate while the woman gave her directions. There was a pizza box on top. *Fresh and delicious. A taste you can't deny.* She must head towards the main road. It would be second on her right.

'Thank you so much.'

She walked off but ignored the woman's directions which had been wrong. Bampton Street was on the left.

Julie was almost back by the university. Her breathing was ragged so she forced herself to slow down, look at the display in the nearest shop. It sold office supplies, but the window was filled with row upon row of masks. These had the faces of celebrities, oddly flattened, with holes for eyes. Scary, but also sad.

As she waited for a bus into town, Julie realised she'd still got that newspaper. Taking one last glance at Bridget, she put her gently in the bin.

Necessary Bandages

C.D. Rose

MADDOX KEEPS HIS NUNS in the attic.

Emmy climbs the stairs, the boards as thin as the tea chests stacked in the hall, banisters like matchsticks. The door hangs half-unhinged, leaking a stink of rotting leaves and damp paper. She treads carefully, worried the squeaking, gibbering floorboards will open up and swallow her. A hole in the roof lets in a gust of cold wet light. She surprises something black (*a crow? a bat?*) which flaps up and out through the hole.

Downstairs the jazz fades, stops, then slowly heaves itself up to speed again.

Pictures in frames as heavy as sadness lean against the raw brick walls. Mottled women and damp-stained men (*dead now,* thinks Emmy) stare lugubriously into the cluttered attic space. One looks like Maddox's mother. Other pictures, pen or print or paint, lie scattered, cruelly ripped from frames or razored from books. Women mostly, ones Maddox had found or stolen, waiting to be snipped up again before being re-membered into collage.

Spattering rain on the roof tiles, mice feet scurrying.

The nuns are nude, and all bald as light bulbs. Some of them are missing arms, or legs, or heads.

Dismembered, she thinks, *or disremembered. What would be the right word?* She wonders if she's drunk too much already: the words won't stay still in her head. Not yet six in the evening

115

but the dark is gathering and she hasn't eaten.

She hears the front door open then close, voices enter, climb the stairs. Voices rise, vie with jazz for volume.

Volumes are stacked in columns on the floor. She crooks her head to read their spines. Engineering. Anatomy. Optics. Books dug from bins, thrown out by students, rescued from the rubbish piles of the old book grubs.

Three black gowns hang on the back of the door. Empty nuns.

Bound with string and crusted with birdshit, a pile of newspapers bears up the eaves, mouldering among arms, legs, and heads. *The paper will soon be dust,* she thinks, *or a sodden mass if the rain gets heavier and that hole never gets fixed.*

A bat, not a crow, it must have been. So different. But both black and flappy. An umbrella. A nun. She'll let Maddox have that; she has no interest in such things.

Pale blue eggshells nestle in the sills. Cobs web between the beams. A bear's paw bears a brass ashtray. The leaves of the books, the leaves of the papers. Bare nuns. Bar none. Words won't stay still.

She pulls up a chair and sticks her head through the hole in the roof. If she tips her toes and stretches she can see Calthorpe Park below, its bare trees sluggard in the grey February cold. Benches sit empty, cast-iron supports and wooden slats awaiting a weary soul's rest. To the left a black trench shoulders the shallow water of the murky River Rea, an iron bridge offering passage across it. Through the spindly branches she can see a row of houses lurking on the opposite side of the park and wonders if someone is peering from an attic roof over there, watching her back. The only things in motion are the slow lights of the traffic on the Pershore Road, soughing past bomb-fronted buildings awaiting demolition or collapse. This is a half-life of a place, where Edgbaston meets Balsall Heath, neither posh nor poor, neither city nor suburb.

She steps back down into the dust which lines the floor more deeply than any carpet. She rolls some between her thumb and forefinger and finds a tiny bone in it. A mouse, maybe, once.

The dust muffles the voices and the jazz downstairs. *It's almost mouse-quiet up here,* she thinks, and she likes that.

She sits on the rickety chair with her back to the door and finds one of the mannequins looking back at her, a nun no longer. She remembers the shop windows in Paris and London, before the war.

'Impressive, aren't they?'

'Jesus, Con, you scared me,' she says, though isn't as surprised by Maddox's appearance as much as by the blasphemy that has come so easily from her mouth. Too much time with these people has changed her words.

'I got them from Greys, on Bull Street, after the bomb.'

'I hope you asked politely.'

'Didn't bother, to be honest. I was prepared to put them all back, I told them so – only with the habits I'd added.'

'That wasn't all, I heard.'

'Detremental to public morals,' he quotes, emphasising the 'e'. 'That's what the bloody council said. Couldn't even spell it right. They're the ones with corrupt minds.'

Emmy doesn't want this discussion again and avoids Maddox's bespectacled glare by staring at a huge moth pinned to the eaves. *Dead already,* she thinks, *though its wings won't decay.* Maddox sees her looking.

'A bobowler. A proper big one.'

She knows the word, doesn't need his gloss. She strokes its dusty wing and it twitches, flies into her face. Not pinned, then. Alive.

'They bring messages from the dead. Only we can't read them,' he laughs. 'I drew pictures of their wings during the war. If you cross moths' wings with umbrellas, I thought, we could be onto something.'

'Surrealism at the service of aviation,' says Emmy.

'I was a draughtsman, a reserved occupation,' says Maddox. 'Surrealism at the service of the nation.'

'We're starting to rhyme.' Rain spatters through the hole. 'Let's go back down. People are arriving.'

'Have you heard about the Count?' Maddox asks on the stairwell, using the darkening hush to speak of secrets. 'Ithell's left him. Or he's left Ithell. Who knows?' She doesn't want to talk about the Count. The Count is past.

Mouse dust sticks to her feet as she pads down the stairs. The boards creak and moan: the long-gone rodent's ghostly voice.

'I don't suppose that's much consolation to you, though.' Maddox is fishing and Emmy won't be fished. Truth is, she doesn't care anymore. Antonio Romanov del Renzio dei Rossi di Castelleone e Venosa seems a long time ago. They all called him the Count. She'd called him Toni.

As they creak down the stairs the scratchy music grows louder, the voices too.

It's been months since she was last here, and the house has grown. The walls are now papered with butchers' wrappers and grocers' bags, seaside postcards, advertising bills, pictures cut from newspapers or torn from books. Maddox has filled any empty space by tracing his own signs and symbols (eyes, scissors, claws) directly onto the plaster. He shows her his room filled with junk, a Wunderkammer of post-war detritus: a massive weaving loom like a mechanical monster, broken-stringed mandolins, nameless farm implements (their purpose unfathomable), horse brasses, old shoes, a mummified cat.

Crossed umbrellas top the living room door, a Surrealist guard of honour. They enter.

Two single mattresses lie in the middle of the floor, and Emmy has no idea why. A four bar heater heats the room, its threadbare flex showing wires like sinews beneath. The smell of burning dust fumes off it. A bearded woman with white, black and brown skin leans against the doorframe, several children, heads shaved louse-free, cluster around her. Emmy tries to count them, loses count. A gramophone, old when her grandmother was young, sits on a plinth blaring scratchy jazz. Emmy sees the needle, the tarnished brass horn. Alongside, a second plinth (marble-stained plywood, rifled from the props dept of an amdram company) bears a typewriter.

Three nuns sit in a row on the sofa.

'Give us a bottle of beer, Con,' says nun one. Not mannequins these, local girls, all their vowels diphthongs: beer becomes *boyer*. Maddox pops bottle tops, hands brown beers to nuns one, two, three.

'We made their habits from blackout curtains,' Maddox tells her. Nun three crosses her legs. Emmy notices Maddox noticing, his bow tie twitching. 'And their knickers from parachute silk!'

He's a little boy, she thinks. *He doesn't know what to do with women.* This obsession with nuns. Trying to understand it, she sees black and white, the strangeness of their clothes, feels the call of a cloistered life.

The brass ashtray, having lost the bear's paw, balances on the arm of the sofa.

A man wearing a top hat arrives. A man with a corduroy jacket and a beard arrives, towing a shadowy girl. Maynard Mitchell, the millionaire brewery heir, arrives with a crate of brown ale. A gypsy goes into the back kitchen.

Top Hat starts to recite a poem, though no one has asked him.

'Knives!' he shouts. 'Forks!'

The bear's paw sits on a low table by the sofa, or perhaps it is another one. A man with an iron foot sidles up to Emmy and tells her the original got eaten by a shark. 'If I ever meet him again, he'll have more trouble with this one!' He wears a great paste jewel around his neck, clasping his collar, and he smells of damp and tobacco (but so does most of this house).

Another nun comes out of the kitchen. Emmy thinks the nun was the gypsy, or perhaps that the gypsy was a nun.

Ironfoot Jack pulls a lacquered Chinese box from his pocket, opens it up and tries to sell her some beads. She's interested.

'Left the orniment at home,' he says. 'Are you anyone's at the moment? You could be mine.' Though they glitter nicely, she turns down the beads.

The nuns smoke, Embassy one, two, three.

'Spoons!' shouts the top-hatted poet. The brass tray fills.

Another new addition, a stuffed barn-owl, sits on a perch by the window where John Melville sits, too, in a great red armchair, tamping leathery tobacco into a pipe.

'Emmy Bridgwater,' he says. 'Always a delight.'

'I didn't hear you come in,' replies Emmy.

'I have always been here, and shall always be here.'

'I thought you and Con had fallen out.'

'Not yet, my dear, not yet.'

Maddox fishes through the dust in the ashtray for burned-out matchsticks and starts to build a tower from them. The tower collapses, they start to divine the meaning of the fallen sticks.

'I didn't think you'd come. Back here. Back to Birmingham,' says Melville. She wonders why she has come. Family pulls like a magnet. To look after her mother, her sister. To paint. She had nowhere else to go.

Another conversation she doesn't want, so she turns her back on Melville and rejoins the room.

'London's done. Paris is done. It's New York now,' says the man in the corduroy jacket.

'Or Birmingham,' says Maddox.

Not here, she thinks, a city smothered by cocoa dust and Quakerism. A thousand trades and none of them hers.

'Mexico,' someone says. Emmy cannot envision Mexico, but thinks of cornmeal earth in a purple night shrill with insects, of thick-scented orchids as big as heads. *Mexico*, she thinks, turning the word over in her head, knowing she will never go there, that it will only ever be a word.

'How's your mother?' asks Maddox, a good man, after all. She doesn't reply because even though she may want to she knows she can't leave: she is a leaf, never falling far, its veins and bones becoming more visible. All that will be left.

The barn-owl turns its head to look at her.

'I'm looking for chess pieces, live ones if possible,' says Maddox to anyone who's listening. 'I want the whole house to be a game of chess.'

'We could live as if it were a game,' says Top Hat, momentarily pausing his poem. 'Throw dice to determine moves. Draw cards. Yes, cards would be better.'

Parlour games, thinks Emmy, mere amusements, and she wants nothing of this silliness. Emmy wants animal bones, birds' eggs, eyes – balls *and* sockets, young girls, leaves, fruit – fresh *and* rotting, open tombs, larvae, rot and rebirth. Night: no, not night, but that moment when day has left and night hasn't come yet, that point where sleep has pitched its house but not yet moved in.

She distracts herself with the typewriter: still Maddox's best work she thinks, the reason she had once thought him a genius. Its keys, instead of bearing letters, each proffer an upturned tack. Now she sees how derivative it is, clever indeed, but little more. His work always reminds her of something else, though she can never quite say what.

'I want it on a real plinth, in Paradise Circus, hard by the Town Hall,' he says to her, to everyone. 'I'll make another version, bigger than Queen Victoria.'

'They'd never have it, you know.'

'Then a curse on sculpture. A curse on statues, a curse on public art. One of these gypsy girls can throw a curse for me.'

'You know very well I'm no gypsy, Conroy Maddox.' Her accent – *pure Kerry,* thinks Emmy. It changes her.

The gaggle of children, brown and white and black, run out for cigarettes and more bottles of brown beer, the millionaire's stock now gone.

People continue to fill the house like smoke. *They are germinating,* thinks Emmy, *generating.* The shadowy girl with hair like a blackout curtain smiles at her but says nothing. A younger man she doesn't know (cardigan, glasses, clean white shirt) proudly shows her a semi-decayed bird carcass, its skeleton newly visible. She takes it into the back kitchen and hangs it, thinking she can strip it later. Two black men, tall, good suits, lean against the counter, and greet her courteously. She sees eggs in a basket, thinks about the bird skull.

A bowl of apples rots on the table.

There are larvae in the thick table legs.

The table rots.

The woman with the beard, whiteblackbrown, comes in, finds a bottle, swats at more children crowding around her, leaves. The men talk between themselves, their voices too low for Emmy to hear.

She goes back into the living room.

'Emmy Bridgwater!' says Melville, rising from his red chair, all forehead. 'How lovely to see you.' She doesn't bother to tell him they had a conversation only a few minutes ago, because she can't really remember if it was only a few minutes ago, or hours ago, or last year. The beer is stronger than she thinks, and perhaps she is drunk, or Melville is drunk, or worse.

'I was having an argument with Con. You must join in.'

'The problem with the London lot was that they never lived in Birmingham,' says Maddox. 'Here, you have to work harder.'

'I found a bunch of bananas on the street the other day,' says Top Hat. 'The surreal is everywhere.' Corduroy disagrees.

'That's not Surrealism, that's comedy.'

'I plan to buy the house next door, and make it solid, just fill it with bricks,' says Maddox.

'You could fix the hole in the roof here, first,' suggests Emmy.

'That's not a hole, that's a passageway.'

The gramophone needle grinds its slow way around the exit groove of the record. No one was listening anyway. Top Hat emerges from the kitchen carrying the cutlery drawer, and tips it all over himself before beginning to sing. Emmy thinks of disembowelling this young man then strangling him with his own entrails: the ultimate Surrealist act.

'Emmy!' says Melville, 'How lovely to see you.'

The room is suddenly very small, and before it gets claustrophobically so, she walks into the back kitchen, which now seems vast. The black men smile. A copper pan on the wall glows in dim light, and she thinks it Maddox's finest ever work before realising that the pan is just a pan. The tap jets cold water. She looks out of the window. Cold white water twists. Top Hat is back in there, trying to kiss a nun.

'Don't worry,' he assures her, 'We'll have forgotten by morning.'

Emmy returns to the living room, now restored to its rightful size and fallen into near silence. Only the hum of the fire, the grind of the record, the hiss of cigarettes.

The girl with the black hair, whose name Emmy never learns, stands by the window where the light is starting to appear. She begins to sing a song about answering an echo, or the echo's answer. Her voice projects like a test tone from the wireless, pure and clear and as direct as the water from the kitchen tap, yet making everything around shiver as though it were no longer solid. The song is full of grace and mystery, an ancient sound broadcast in from the future. She seems uncertain of her voice, as if it were possessing her: the song singing the singer, a mere transmitter. Emmy is transfixed. As the girl sings, everything other than the low hisses and hums of the clicks of the room around her fall quiet. Her voice echoes itself into the end of the song, there is a fizz of electricity, a clank in the street outside, birdsong. Then silence.

The work of the night is done.

'We'll all be forgotten by morning,' says one of the black guys walking through the hallway. As they leave, Emmy wonders who they are, but no one knows.

I do not know who they are. I've looked in books, talked to people, searched libraries and websites, but can find nothing. I want to know who they are, and the unnamed women too. I cannot believe the nuns were ever really nuns, nor the gypsies Romany or Irish Travellers. I hope they appear somewhere in Janet Mendelsohn's late 1960s *Varna Road* photographs which document the area so well, but I cannot see them. They could still be alive, out there somewhere. While others present have had their exhibitions and monographs, no one can identify these people. But when they leave Conroy Maddox's Surrealist gathering, late on a cold February night in 1951, they walk out of history. At which point, for a moment, so do we.

★

Half a life ago I lived in Birmingham; half a life later I came back.

Time had been kind to the city, in its way: it seemed to have thickened and slowed to the point of near-stoppage, trudged on by a few minutes for each decade.

And yet, between my departure and my return the city had erected and destroyed several other iterations of itself. Builders had shifted their hands to tearing down that which they had not long completed. Birmingham is a true city of the future: endlessly becoming, never arriving.

At Paradise Circus, where Emmy Bridgwater had a studio, they build knowing they will demolish. In a cold February in 2018, when I write this, there isn't a passageway, just a hole. Nearby, Antony Gormley's *Iron:Man* and Gillian Wearing's *A Real Birmingham Family* have been removed into an obscure and indefinite storage; Raymond Mason's *Forward* was burned into an unrecognisable mass by kid vandals fifteen years back.

The centre of the modern city stretches from the Alpha Tower to the omega of the Rotunda, its omphalos the now-vanished library. Between these points the small group of Birmingham Surrealists met and argued: at the Kardomah Café on the corner of New Street and Needless Alley, its sign still just visible; at the Trocadero, now showing Sky Sports and serving two-for-one cocktails from five till eight. I try to find Maddox's house but Speedwell Road has been interrupted, its lower half replaced by a low-rise housing estate.

*

When Maddox and Melville are finally alone, snoring on the sofa, Emmy creeps out into a morning as pale and as brave as the girl whose song she will try and paint. It's a good walk from here to her studio, but it matters little. She has work to do.

About the Contributors

Balvinder Banga grew up in Handsworth, Birmingham before going on to read Law at Cambridge University. In a varied career, he has practiced as a barrister, served in the British Army and now works for an NGO in India. He has published in various journals including *South Asian Popular Culture* and *Wasafiri* (in its 30th anniversary edition), and came third in Cinnamon Press's 2016 annual short story competition.

Alan Beard writes stories and flash fiction. He has published two collections *Taking Doreen out of the Sky* (Picador, 1999) and *You Don't Have to Say* (Tindal Street Press, 2010). He won the Tom-Gallon award for best short story, and his work has been broadcast on BBC Radio 4 and appeared in *Best British Short Stories 2011* (Salt) and *Best Short Stories* (Heinemann, 1991), as well as in numerous UK, US and Canadian magazines.

Jendella Benson is a British-Nigerian writer, photographer and filmmaker, who grew up in Birmingham and is now based in London. Her work has appeared in *The Guardian, BuzzFeed, MTV News UK,* and *Metro,* amongst many others. She is the contributing editor at *Black Ballad* and is also a TEDx speaker with appearances on BBC Radio 4, London Live and OH TV. Jendella's book, *Young Motherhood*, was published in May 2017.

Kavita Bhanot's fiction, non-fiction and reviews have been published and broadcast widely. She is Editor of the anthology *Too Asian, Not Asian Enough* (Tindal Street Press 2011) and co-editor of the *Bare Lit anthology* (Brain Mill Press, 2017). She is a Leverhulme Early Career Fellow at Leicester University. She has been selected as a 2018 Room 204 writer by Writing West Midlands and has been shortlisted for the SI Leeds Literary Prizei. She s a reader and mentor with The Literary Consultancy.

Kit de Waal was born in Birmingham to an Irish mother and a Caribbean father. She worked for fifteen years in criminal and family law, was a magistrate for several years. Her writing has received numerous awards including the Bridport Flash Fiction Prize 2014 and 2015, the SI Leeds Literary Reader's Choice Prize 2014 and the Kerry Group Irish Novel of the Year. Her works include *My Name is Leon* (Penguin, 2016) and *The Trick to Time* (Viking, 2018)

Sharon Duggal is a writer, campaigner and broadcaster. Her acclaimed debut novel, *The Handsworth Times* (Bluemoose Books, 2016) was *The Morning Star's* fiction 'Book of the Year 2016' and the chosen title for Brighton City Reads 2017. Sharon is the 2018 Writer in Residence at Creative Future and is the recipient of an Arts Council England award.

Joel Lane was a novelist, short story writer, poet and critic. He was the author of four collections of supernatural horror stories (*Where Furnaces Burn, The Earth Wire, The Lost District* and *The Terrible Changes*) plus a weird novella and three collections of poems. He also edited an anthology of subterranean horror tales (*Beneath the Ground*) and co-edited an anthology of urban crime and suspense stories (*Birmingham Noir,* with Steve Bishop) and an anthology of weird and speculative fiction stories against racism and fascism (*Never Again,* with Allyson Bird). He received the World Fantasy Award in 2013 and the British Fantasy Award twice.

Malachi McIntosh was born in Birmingham but raised in the United States. He worked for five years in academia after completing a PhD in English, but stepped down from a post at Cambridge in June 2016 to focus on writing full time. His work has been published in *Broadcast, The Caribbean Review of Books, Flash: The International Short-Short Story Magazine, Fugue, The Guardian* and *Wasafiri*. He was the 2014 recipient of the David Higham Writing Award at UEA and is a 2018/19 participant of Writing West Midlands' Room 204 Programme.

Bobby Nayyar was born in Handsworth, Birmingham in 1979. He read French and Italian at Trinity College, Cambridge, and Comparative Literature at the University of Chicago. He has been published in *Mango Shake* and *Too Asian, Not Asian Enough* anthologies, and journals, including *Wasafiri, Aesthetica* and *The Woven Tale Press*. He founded Limehouse Books in 2009, publishing his debut novel, *West of No East* in 2011, and *The No Salaryman* two years later. In 2016, he published his debut poetry collection, *Glass Scissors*, which received a Word Masala award. He lives in London. @bobbynayyar

C.D. Rose has written stories set in Paris, Naples, St. Petersburg, Lisbon, Manchester and Birmingham. Some of these have been published in *Best British Stories 2018, Gorse, The Lonely Crowd* and *Lighthouse* magazines, and Comma's *Parenthesis* anthology. Most recently, he is the author of *Who's Who When Everyone Is Someone Else* (Melville House, 2018).

Sibyl Ruth is the author of two small press collections of poetry and is a former Poet Laureate of Birmingham. She has also translated poetry written by her German great aunt, Rose Scooler about the Terezin Ghetto. She works in the city's community libraries.

ALSO AVAILABLE IN THE
'READING THE CITY' SERIES...

The Book of Dhaka
Edited by Arunava Sinha & Pushpita Alam

The Book of Gaza
Edited by Atef Abu Saif

The Book of Havana
Edited by Orsola Casagrande

The Book of Istanbul
Edited by Jim Hinks & Gul Turner

The Book of Khartoum
Edited by Raph Cormack & Max Shmookler

The Book of Leeds
Edited by Tom Palmer & Maria Crossan

The Book of Liverpool
Edited by Maria Crossan & Eleanor Rees

The Book of Riga
Edited by Becca Parkinson & Eva Eglaja-Kristsone

The Book of Rio
Edited by Toni Marques & Katie Slade

The Book of Tbilisi
Edited by Becca Parkinson & Gvantsa Jobava

The Book of Tokyo
Edited by Jim Hinks, Masashi Matsuie
& Michael Emmerich